TORTURED

The Mercenary Series

SUZANNE E. LANG

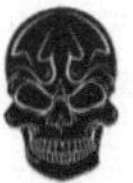

CHAPTER ONE

"Your brother is missing."

In the midst of sparring with her foster mother, Steph hesitated, just for a second, as she digested the announcement. The pause meant she was quickly punished as her teacher landed a blow to her midsection, knocking the air from her.

What little air she had left, that was. Her mind still reeled from the news.

"What do you mean he's missing?" she managed to reply as she held up her arms to block a flurry of blows.

Zola, her guardian, foster mother, and woman who didn't believe in bullshitting or pussyfooting replied, "Are you hard of hearing? Do you require a dictionary? He's missing, as in no one has seen or heard from him in over a week."

A week! "Why am I just finding this out now?"

"Because we wanted to be sure Ronin hadn't just gone dark because of his mission."

By mission, Zola meant Ronin's job for their benefactor. A job he wouldn't divulge no matter how much she prodded him. Stupid, protective older brother jerk thought he could keep her safe by keeping her in the dark.

"Is he dead?" She had a hard time getting the stiff words past her lips. *He can't be dead.* They'd been through too much together for him to leave her now.

"I don't think so."

"Don't this so?" She might have screeched. "What the fuck kind of bullshit—"

Zola interrupted her. "Zip it right now before I zip it for you. Hysteria won't accomplish anything."

"How can you be so calm about this?"

"Who says I'm calm?"

Outwardly, Zola appeared just as stoic as usual—her mahogany skin only holding trace lines of age and no crease of worry, her braids held back with a leather thong. Her eyes, though, stormed. Their striking green color a tempest at sea.

"We have to find him. Call out the boys. We'll mount a rescue expedition." A posse of ne'er do wells that would sweep the islands in search of her brother.

"Easy nuh," Zola said, her island accent thick. "We ain't doin' nothing…"

"Fuck you. I am not sitting here on my ass while he's out there maybe needing my help."

"We dunno what he needs. Or if he needs it, and until we do…" The green gaze narrowed. "You will show respect, little *dawta*." That was the only warning Steph got before her foster mum resumed their sparring lesson.

Although, these days it was less a lesson and more like exercise. Years of practice meant Steph no longer ended up on her back gasping for breath, or sporting bruises the length of her body.

The reminder brought her mind into focus and she spent the next few minutes blocking shots, leaning Matrix-style away from a sweeping foot, dropping to the ground and kicking out with her own.

Fists moving rapidly, she landed a hit and got a tight smile. "Better."

With that slight praise, she felt confident enough to ask, "What is being done to find Ronin?" Because unlike other gangs that sent out their soldiers and wiped their hands clean if they failed, the mercenary group—aka orphanage for lost children—that saved Steph and Ronin took care of their own.

"Nuthin' being done yet. Count yourself lucky I told you. The boss man was wanting to keep it a secret."

Her lips pressed into a tight line. "Why?"

A shrug of Zola's broad shoulders went with her reply. "Because he didn't want you gettin' all crazy and running off doing something foolish."

"Me, do something crazy?"

Zola snorted. She knew Steph all too well.

"Obviously you think differently or you wouldn't have told me. So, what do you expect me to do?" Going off half cocked, driven by an emotional need, wouldn't go over well. Henderson expected his bandulus to follow the rules. It was part of the promise they made when he brought them in off the alleys and streets. Break them and you might not be allowed to return. You would be considered outcast.

Despite her sense of urgency to find Ronin, Steph wasn't ready to lose the only family she'd ever known. *But, I also can't lose my brother.*

Assuming a fighting stance, Zola bounced on the balls of her feet. "We could do nuthin'. Your brother is a right hot-stepper with the mad skills to get himself out of trouble."

"Unless he's run into something bigger than he can handle."

"Then he might be fucked."

The very thought made Steph see red. She lunged, but Zola blocked the shot and countered, the stinging blow hard enough to leave a bruise. Angry, and out of control, Steph didn't even realize she was crying until the tears made her vision too blurry to see.

"What's with the waters, dawta?"

"He's my brother."

"Ya wanna chase down his ass?"

"What do you think?" Steph drawled, scrubbing at the hot tears with the back of her hand. "If he's really in trouble then every minute counts."

"And what if Mr. H done goes and says no?"

Could she go against the man who had given her so much?

For Ronin, she'd do anything. "He's my brother. I have to do something."

Zola's lips curved into a smile as she nodded. "I agree. Which is why, despite your many shortcomings, dawta, I suggested to the big bossman himself that you be in charge of hunting Ronin down."

"Me?" The unexpected suggestion caused Steph to pause. As she stood there dumbstruck, her sensei kicked, her foot lunging out and hooking around her ankle, dumping Steph on her ass.

She landed hard, losing all the air in her lungs, but

that was nothing compared to the gasping in her mind as she realized what her teacher implied.

"You think I'm ready." Ready to be more than a student. Ready for more than just running petty errands and doing mundane tasks for the orphan bandulus. *Finally ready to do my part.*

"I doubt you're ready. None of you dumbfucks ever is, but you deserve a chance to fuck up like everyone else."

"I never asked for special protection." Most of the orphans, once they hit a certain age, went on to work for Henderson via one of his many branches. The orphanage run by Zola and a few other adults, kept a steady stream of loyal bandulus to fill in the gaps as folks retired—or died. Life wasn't easy in the islands.

Until now, Zola kept holding Steph back. Mostly because of Ronin. Her stupid older brother kept claiming she wasn't ready. Wasn't strong enough.

Being the smallest person in the gang, plus a woman to boot, meant Steph had to work twice as hard. Fight twice as dirty.

Heaving herself off the hard ground—because training on mats was for pussies—she threw herself at Zola and wrapped her arms around the big woman. Bigger than most men, and muscled too. Zola was the one who found a teenage boy and his baby sister in an alley scrounging for scraps. The one who decided the pale-skinned Americans abandoned in the islands should become part of their misfit family. The one who told her that tears were for sissies and that big girls didn't cry. They got even.

"I wouldn't get excited yet. If we're going, then

we're gonna be stuck on the *Petit Poisson*." The smallest ship they had in their rag tag fleet.

"We?" A smile curved Steph's lips as she pulled away from her foster mum.

"Yes we." Zola snorted. "You didn't really think I'd let my dawta's scrawny ass go off by itself, did you? Someone's got to keep you out of trouble."

Funny, because all the stories she heard had Zola starting it.

"When do we leave?"

"Now, unless you got something more important to do."

"Where are we going?" Brimming with questions, Steph shadowed her teacher as she took off at a brisk walk toward the compound.

Her excitement at leaving almost managed to balance her worry about her brother. On the one hand, she understood Ronin's situation must be dire if Zola was willing to leave the compound and go looking. But at the same time, Steph only rarely left its confines, the gang—and most especially her brother—keeping her protected at its bosom, the unofficial little sister and daughter of every mercenary both young and old that passed through.

"I know his last known location. Even his last contact. We'll start with him. So pack your bag, dawta, and get ready to get dirty because that tiny ship won't sail itself."

"I won't let you down."

"You'd better not or I'll throw you overboard myself." Zola would. Steph had seen her do it once with a young punk who thought he could mouth off.

A few fins coasting nearby and a shark brushing past him in the water taught that boy proper respect.

"Am I going to have to fight, do you think?" Until now, she'd only tested her skills against other orphans and Zola. She looked forward to seeing how she did in the real world.

"More than likely."

"And probably kill." The reality of the bandulus included murder as a fact of life. Only the strongest survived. She knew that, but the reality of it was another thing. Did she have what it took to administer that final deadly blow?

She had no doubt that killing a person would prove a lot different than the killing stroke to the wild boar that roamed the jungles or the rats that liked to infiltrate the cold cellar.

"You will do whatever you must to stay alive. What's the first rule I taught you?" Zola's gaze pierced her.

"Cry babies don't get dinner."

Her foster mum's lips twitched. "Second rule then."

"If it's not on your side, kill it."

"Exactly. You can't afford to be squeamish or soft. Out there it's kill or be killed."

"I won't let you down."

"You'd better not. Or I'll hunt your little ass down in the afterlife." Zola glared, but Steph recognized it for her version of affection.

"We're really doing this, aren't we?" Her heart fluttered with anticipation."

"Aye, we are."

"Will you kill me if I squeal?"

A scowl pulled Zola's lips. "I will if you hug me

again." Contrary to the media portrayal of black women as caregivers, Zola wasn't a cuddly Aunt Jemima type. She was a fierce and strong woman. Someone Steph looked up to and loved. Which was why she hugged her anyhow.

And Zola cursed her out. "Stupid, clingy girl child. What is wrong with you?"

Wrong? She'd gone from despair to hope. There was no use crying over the things she couldn't change. Only act and do the best she could.

Steph laughed, a bright sound that carried through the compound and brought a few looks from the boys training in the yard. But never anything more than looks because everyone knew Steph was off limits.

If her brother didn't maim them, then Zola would. No one touched her *dawta*.

With a whoop and a fist pump, Steph bolted for her room to fix herself a bag because, knowing Zola, they wouldn't waste any time before departing.

It didn't take long to pack the essentials. Life in the compound didn't allow for frivolous extras. Just spare clothes, toiletries, and her knife, the one given years ago to her on her eighteenth birthday by her brother. He'd had the handle carved with their motto: *Fuck the world, you and me, sis.*

And those words were why she would find his ass, and save it. Because she owed him her life.

___

CHAPTER TWO

___

Would it kill me to say no for once?

As Gavin stared at the hulking, almost eight foot thug he'd agreed to fight, he had to wonder if perhaps he'd finally gotten one concussion too many.

Just once, couldn't he have let an insult slide? Or turn down the offer of easy money? Say no to a triple dog dare?

The question was kind of moot seeing as how he'd already gotten himself caught up in a situation. A really large situation. *What possessed me to agree to take on this beast?*

The pot of money at the end would prove hard to spend if he ended up in traction. It wasn't as if he needed more cash. Smuggling was a lucrative business, mercenary for hire even more so, and he had the bulging bank accounts to prove it.

As for his reputation, it didn't need any help. People knew him. Respected him. Avoided him on the street.

Most people, at any rate. His old chum Cole only laughed when Gavin drunkenly told him to "Respect my authority." Of course, it might have had more panache if he'd not belched at the end.

So, if Gavin didn't need fame or fortune, then why the fuck was he about to step into a makeshift dirt ring with a guy whose mother obviously fed him steroids with her breastmilk?

Boredom was partially to blame, as was the flask he'd sucked back. But more to the point, Gavin agreed to fight because his buddies—and sometimes partners in crime—Gunner and Lash dared him.

"Hundred bucks says Gavin gets his ass handed to him within the first sixty seconds," Lash had said, his brown eyes twinkling.

Hair swept off his forehead in a style some women found attractive, Gunner shook his head. "He's fast enough to dodge those skull crushers for a few minutes. I say he gets KO'd somewhere between the three and four minute mark."

Being a man with balls intact—a quick scratch confirmed their presence—Gavin declared, "Fuck both of you. Five hundred bucks says I can take his ass and lay him flat."

"You're on."

The wager accepted meant Gavin had no choice. Real men didn't back down from a challenge. But perhaps he should think about getting his head checked.

The fight was being held behind the tavern—because so many good decisions came out of a place that served copious amounts of booze. The hard packed dirt had long since been scrubbed free of grass. Only a few brave weeds, their roots fed by all the shed blood, dared to grow through the stained earth.

There were no ropes here, or fancy bells and electronic scoreboards. Just a circle of men and women, rough-looking for the most part, jostling for position, many wanting to get close enough to feel the spray of sweat.

Those that considered themselves more genteel tended to watch from the balcony. The rich preferred not to get their suits spattered with blood, or get caught in an accidental melee when the crowd went wild.

This wasn't a sanctioned fight like that shit you saw on television with hyper announcers and referees. There were no rules here except one: Don't die.

Stripping off his shirt, Gavin tossed it at Lash, who didn't bother to uncross his arms, letting the fabric fall to the ground.

"I'll need that later," Gavin remarked.

Not bothering to look down, Lash shrugged. "Maybe. Maybe not. Either way, I ain't holding it for you."

Prick. Then again, Gavin would have said the same thing.

Upper body bared, Gavin limbered his muscles, stretching his arms forward, then back. Overhead and twisting. He put his body through a series of warm ups, prepping his muscles.

Something cold and viscous hit his back, and he whirled with a snarl. "What the fuck, asshole?"

Gunner grinned. "Just making you slippery so Meathead over there can't grab you too easily and crush you to a pulp."

"Your confidence overwhelms," was Gavin's dry reply.

"Don't be such a whine-bag," Lash retorted. "You should be thanking us. The oil will make your skin shine for the ladies watching. Just be careful you rinse off before you let them ride you cowgirl style. I lost a rider that way. Had a hard time explaining it to the coppers."

The mental image of a woman flying off during coitus didn't put Gavin in the right mindset. Chuckling before a match wasn't manly.

Think of violent things, like punching him out when this is done.

"Do me a favor, and stay out of this," he demanded.

"Does this mean you don't want us to help if it looks like Meathead is gonna pop your head like a pimple?"

Again, an image he could have done without, especially since he'd gotten a glimpse of Meathead's huge hands. "No one is popping my head today."

"Said no man ever," Lash snickered. "If that blonde in the red dress offers, I'll let her suck me for free." He winked at someone on the second floor.

"As if she'd want to blow you," Gunner retorted. "A fine honey like that wants a man of refinement like me." He blew a kiss that resulted in Lash shoving him, which led to some tussling.

"Are you assholes done yet?" Gavin asked.

The guys stopped and acted as if they'd not just gotten into another fight. For best friends, it happened an awful lot.

"Is he always this pissy before a match?" Gunner asked.

"It's on account he's getting old," Lash said with a sage nod of his head, at odds with his youthful appearance.

The alcohol wearing off meant weariness began to set in. Couldn't have that before a fight, so Gavin decided to work on amping his irritation and punched

Lash in the gut, not the face, because dude was freaking tall.

It didn't even make the blockhead flinch.

Lash canted his head. "I hope that wasn't your best shot."

"Of course it wasn't," blustered Gunner. "Fucker is keeping his best shit and energy for the fight, right? Please tell me you can hit harder than that. Maybe I should change my wager." Gunner rubbed his chin.

"It was pretty soft. My mother slaps me harder," Lash admitted.

At Gavin's pointed glare, both guys laughed.

"You assholes aren't funny," Gavin growled through gritted teeth. "But you apparently have a death wish because when I finish this fight—"

"Don't you mean if?" Gunner interjected.

"*When*," he emphasized, "I'm done, I'm going to find your sorry asses and beat you two within an inch of your lives."

"The boy thinks he's gonna walk away from this," Lash snickered.

Gunner grinned. "He'll be lucky if he can pass out in a bed. Don't worry. If you can't perform a winning round for the ladies, I'll take your place."

"You? What about me?" Lash protested.

"You can have my sloppy seconds."

"How about you suck my dick?" Lash snarled, grabbing his crotch. "Better yet, choke on it."

"How about you both keep your dicks in your pants."

"Seems like a waste of some good dicks, if you ask me." Gunner peered down at his groin and Gavin could only roll his eyes.

Stupid fuckers never took a damned thing seriously. Probably why he enjoyed their company so much—and wanted to kill them in equal measure.

"I'm going to expect a bottle of something that is almost one hundred percent alcohol when I'm done."

"Get you drunk. On it," Lash announced.

More like Lash would need it to pour it on his wounds because this was gonna hurt.

A guy with a bullhorn shouted, "Fighters, take your places. And the rest of you zip it."

The clamor died down as Gavin stepped into the makeshift ring formed by crowded bodies.

As the ring master bellowed some profanity to get the crowd riled, Gavin sized up his opponent.

Bigger and uglier up close than expected, the thug Lash nicknamed Meathead wasn't a believer in bathing or deodorant. The heavy reek of jerk spice and garlic, along with the distinct stench of ball sweat would fell a lesser man.

Don't fear the fist, fear the infection all that bacteria will cause.

I must be getting old if I'm worried about germs. In his early thirties, he shouldn't already have such curmudgeonly thoughts.

Keeping his gaze trained on his opponent, Gavin searched for any signs of weakness. Did the guy favor one side over the other? Did that scar on his knee indicate an old injury he could exploit?

The guy on the bullhorn finally got to the introductions. "To my left, we've got the house champion, Crusher, undefeated now for three years running."

Undefeated? How had he not heard this tidbit? Then again, Gavin usually didn't frequent these types of base taverns. At his age, he preferred a more sophisticated atmosphere that didn't serve drinks out of cloudy chipped glasses and where passing out didn't mean you'd end up waking in the alley naked, with a greasy ass.

"To my right, we've got his puny opponent. A local smuggler known for navigating the waters and giving the middle finger to pirates, Gavin 'Crusty Seadog.'"

What the fuck was this Crusty Seadog shit? A dart of his eyes showed Lash grinning broadly. No need to look further for the culprit.

The nickname didn't sit well with him mostly because he knew a sleaze ball who used that moniker. As if he wanted his brand associated with that small time thug.

With a hoarse holler of, "Let's see some blood," the fight commenced.

The roar of the crowd deafened, a wave of sound obliterating everything in its path. The many bodies perfumed the space, making it even more odiferous than usual. The air hung heavy and humid. The distractions proved numerous, and yet Gavin forced himself to remain focused on one thing.

Staying alive.

He bobbed on the balls of his feet, doing a slow circle of the ring, taking Meathead's measure. The big guy didn't seem in a hurry, he played to the crowd, grinning toothlessly at them, slapping one closed fist into his palm.

Gavin probably imagined the tremble of the earth each time the big fucker moved. He didn't let it intimidate. Size didn't mean shit—unless you were in bed. Then a big dick could save a guy lots of tongue work.

But in the ring, bigger might mean more powerful, but it also meant slower, and easily tired.

Usually.

There were exceptions.

The first swing of a fist arrived in slow motion, or so it seemed to Gavin who'd dropped in to the zone. Those who fought knew what he talked about, it was a quiet space where the crowd, the noise, everything faded into nothingness and the only thing left was the fight.

Gavin easily dodged the fist and the second jabbing shot. Seeing an opening, he threw a punch of his own, only to see it blocked, the unyielding wall of muscle he hit sending a shockwave through his arm.

Solid guy. Pummeling his opponent into submission didn't seem likely. Hell, even if Gavin had a knife, he might find it hard to sink it deep enough past the muscle to do any harm. His only hope was to tire the beast out and find a sloppy opening.

With a plan in place, Gavin went to work.

"Hey, Meathead," he called out. "I hear your wife's been complaining." He ducked and bounced back up. "Something about the 'roids shrinking your dick. Maybe you should just admit to her that your small penis is a result of your small brain."

The other fellow gargled something that sprayed spit. Gross. Gavin caught most of it on an upraised arm then bit back a gasp as a solid blow rocked him.

"You call that a hit," he taunted, still dancing on the balls of his feet. "My mother used to slap me harder. Hell, I tapped your old lady harder last night in bed. You should have heard her singing 'Like a Virgin.'"

"Rawr." More inarticulate noise as Meathead

charged at him. Gavin pretended to flourish a cape and yanked himself out of the way el matador style.

The crowd went wild. So did the big guy.

Meathead charged again and Gavin kept taunting. "Don't feel bad about your old lady cheating. You can do better than that twat. Like your momma. Boy, she knows how to suck."

Dirty. Low. Effective.

The big guy chased Gavin around the ring. Not that Gavin just dodged and ran. He sometimes ducked to end up behind the guy, kicking at the backs of his knees. Other times he'd whirl and let him get close only to duck before a pulverizing fist, again using his quickness to jab at any soft spots he could find. There weren't many.

But, good news, the big fucker was tiring. He panted. Sweated even more than seemed possible.

Having kept count in his head, and being a bit of a dick, Gavin turned at this point to shout to his buddies, "Hey, losers, get ready to cough up the dough."

Because he was going to collect.

Knowing the end neared, Gavin added some flourish to his movements. This was, after all, a show, and the crowd needed to be fed. Lash and Gunner hadn't exaggerated when they said the ladies were watching.

Then again, ladies was a bit of a misnomer. Any woman wearing a dress that left nothing to the imagination and enough makeup to make her unrecognizable even to her mother was no lady.

But definitely a good time in bed.

One broad in the front row in particular caught his eye, mostly because, unlike the other women, she wasn't wearing anything skimpy. Her snug t-shirt outlined her breasts and actually went to her waist. She wore no makeup at all, and her reddish hair was caught back in a ponytail. Not exactly the usual island tart, and yet she eyeballed him with vast interest.

He proffered a panty dropping smile.

She arched a brow and smirked.

He looked forward to turning that smirk into—

Whack.

Inattention cost him, rattling his jaw and making him curse his cock. Now was not the time to eyeball the prospects.

There'd be plenty of time to choose a lucky haven for his cock after the fight.

Then after he'd fucked her—or she fucked him cross-eyed—he'd catch up with Lash and Gunner. And by catch up, he meant knock their asses unconscious and smuggle them onto a freighter with supplies for the Antarctic.

In his world, it was all about priorities and getting even.

Still, priorities didn't mean he didn't take a second to wink at the redhead still watching him. He might have also mouthed, "Me, you, later."

Now to get to the later part without dying because Meathead, beating his chest and roaring King Kong-like for the enjoyment of the crowd, had found his second wind.

CHAPTER THREE

Did he just wink at me?

Surely not. She peeked behind her but saw only screaming men, their eyes wide and wild, their mouths gaping holes shouting encouragement and obscenities.

Foul language didn't bother her. Having grown up in the orphanage around boys who tended to have rough edges, she'd heard it all. What she wasn't prepared for was her fascination with the man fighting in the ring.

The very sexy guy.

She'd seen half naked dudes before. Tons of them. Yet, none had ever made her heart race, her mouth go dry, or given her the urge to rub her hands over his skin.

The guy in the ring evoked that and more.

From the moment she'd seen him, she'd found herself riveted. Then again, there was good reason.

He was an incredible fighter.

At first, when they'd pitted him against the behemoth, she'd thought like everyone else that he'd get clobbered—thus quickly ending her quest for answers.

But he proved them wrong. Fleet of foot, he

possessed strength, dexterity, and an uncanny ability to predict when and where to dodge.

Zola often said you could teach someone the basics of fighting, but you couldn't teach instinct.

This man flowed when he moved. His oiled muscles rippled as he contorted and swayed in ways that should have been impossible. So many times she held her breath, certain he was about to get pulverized, and yet, each time, he managed to escape and dance away. Except when she caught his gaze.

For a moment they'd stared at each other. Shared a strange instant amidst the chaos.

Then he got smoked by a fist and she winced for him. Luckily, one powerful blow wasn't enough to put him down. The man they called Crusty Seadog bounced back stronger than ever, captivating her and pissing off the crowd who'd apparently wagered against him.

"Fuck me, the little bastard is gonna win," grumbled a fellow to her left.

It sure looked that way, and that excited her. Not just because she needed to speak with him. The guy, the man, the hunk of toned flesh, excited her.

She hoped her hard nipples didn't show through her t-shirt. Thank God her jeans would hide the wetness in her pussy.

Steph was attracted to him. A veritable stranger. He actually got her motor purring.

A pity nothing would ever happen. The man in the ring was a means to an end. A clue in the puzzle of her missing brother. She wouldn't allow attraction to get in the way of her goal.

Of course, her goal might be hampered if he died.

The guy surely suffered some kind of mental deficiency. Who voluntarily pitted themselves against a giant?

Someone with huge freaking balls, that's who.

Even cloistered as she was in the compound, she'd heard of Crusher. Undefeated champion, and not by knock out. A guy who killed all who opposed him. Challenging him was tantamount to a death sentence.

Was Gavin, the Crusty Seadog, suicidal? Perhaps he was feeling guilt over his many crimes.

Was he guilty of hurting her brother?

Her gaze narrowed. He'd better not have. She wouldn't suffer from any conscience if that was the case.

A firm blow sent Seadog flying, the fist literally lifting him off the ground and knocking him back a few feet.

For a moment, it appeared as if he might not get up. The big dude certainly thought so and celebrated too quickly as he stomped over to the prone body. Lightning quick, Gavin reared up, feet lashing out and connecting with the giant's nuts.

To those who might cry foul, shut the fuck up. In a battle where death was the outcome, there existed no such thing as a dirty move. Only survival.

He'd better survive.

She'd spent two days on the mainland looking for clues. Two days of retracing Ronin's steps—into brothels and other places that left her feeling dirty. *Why would my brother stoop to paying for sex?* Not that any of the ladies admitted to servicing him. They only recalled seeing a tall, tattooed guy coming in.

It made no sense. Ronin could have his pick of any woman.

Perhaps it was part of his mission for Henderson?

Undeterred, she waylaid strangers in alleys, and used the tip of her knife to demand answers.

No one had any. Ronin's location eluded her and her patience waxed thin.

And then, out of nowhere, a lucky break. The beady-eyed rat she'd cornered last night had said something about a tattooed guy meeting with a low level thug who belonged to a rival gang. A scumbag known for double dealings.

Crusty Seadog.

Just a single name. No address. So where was he staying in town? The place was huge. Ramshackle buildings and shanties for parts of it, mansions and gleaming condos for others. Despite the dark underworld, tourism thrived. Throngs of people roamed the streets.

Finding one man on a barebones description of dark hair in the midst of it all was almost impossible, until she overhead a pair of fellows mention something about a dare and the name she'd almost given up hope on. Apparently, they'd entered Crusty Seadog into a fight.

This fight.

Wham. The roundhouse kick staggered the larger man. Another followed, then a rapid blur of punches as Gavin—*how the hell did he end up with a scummy name like Crusty Seadog?*—feigning fatigue, attacked the tired giant.

Blow after blow landed, so fast the giant never had a chance to recover. He fell, tripped by a hooked foot and a shove.

The man she'd come seeking had some mad skills, and she wouldn't mind pitting herself against him. Testing herself against his strength and ability.

Naked.

What?

The stray thought caused her to gasp a moment before the crowd joined her as Gavin dropped an elbow onto the guy on the ground. A sudden arm block prevented the deadly blow and then they were at it again.

But she had hope now that he would win, and be tired afterwards. It would make her plan easier. Her usual submission moves might not work on Gavin were he rested and at full strength.

As a woman in a man's world, she knew her limitations. However, Steph had more than just her bare hands to help her. Zola had equipped her with a few tools.

As the giant went down for a second time, Gavin didn't hesitate. Gripping the giant's head, he gave it a rapid flick, effectively snapping the neck and killing the bigger man instantly.

The crowd *Ooohed*, a few grumbled, but no one was truly angry. The giant wouldn't have hesitated to end Gavin if the roles were reversed.

The best fighter won.

Little did he know he was about to be bested by a woman.

CHAPTER FOUR

I DID IT. GAVIN WOULD LIVE TO REGRET HIS POOR choices another day. He did his best to not let his aching body and fatigue show as he strutted from the ring into the tavern for a victory drink.

To the left of him, Lash sang "We Are The Champions" off key but enthusiastically.

There was no we about it. I kicked ass.

Again.

Really, sometimes he had to wonder why he bothered. Where was the challenge? Where had the thrill gone? Because he felt nothing.

No true elation, no sense of accomplishment. Just another fight, one that left him richer, his reputation fiercer than ever—and his body aching from contusions.

I'm getting too old for this shit.

The shot of whiskey went down like fire, burning its way through him, pushing back some of the pain, while doing nothing for the bloody cut above his eye. That needed more than a napkin doused in rum to fix it.

"You kicked ass out there," Gunner said, slapping

him on the back, right over a developing bruise. He bit back a wince.

Yup, way too old for this shit.

"You should have seen their faces when you took him down." Lash chuckled. "I thought one dude was gonna cry. He'd wagered his paycheck on the fight. His old lady is gonna kill him."

"She should." Only a moron would wager against Gavin. Then again, when was the last time he'd pitted his skills in a ring?

A while. Probably because the last time he got stupid he spent a few weeks nursing the aftermath.

Maybe it's time I took it easy. Maybe retired from the mercenary life.

"Retire?" Said with astonishment.

Shit, had he spoken aloud? "Why not? I've got money. A place to call my own." His long standing feud with Cole was a thing of the past and he knew Henderson was on the lookout for guys to run the office part of the operations. Why not him?

"But what about the excitement?"

"The women," Lash exclaimed.

"Yes, the women," Gunner repeated.

The truth tumbled out and he blamed the whiskey. "I'm tired of different pussy every night."

He deserved the slap Lash gave him as he exclaimed, "What the fuck are you saying? Did Meathead scramble your brains? Variety of pussy is the spice of life."

"It's like desserts. Yes, you can love one for a while, but really, why would you settle for tasting just one sweet treat when you can have a buffet?" Gunner explained.

"Yeah, you're right," Gavin said because it was

easier to agree. Out loud at any rate. In his head, though?

*I think I'm ready for something different. Something—*gasp*—monogamous.*

A shocking change of mind especially since, until recently, Gavin used to think more pussy was better. Then he saw Cole and his chick Lillie together. Saw the tight bond they'd formed, the love they had for one another, and fuck him, but he envied it.

Envied his friend for having someone he wanted to settle down with and start a family. Someone to call his own.

One woman for life.

Madness.

"It's the adrenaline crash talking." Lash slapped him on the back and Gavin did his best not to turn around and slug his friend.

Show no pain.

"Don't worry, old friend, we'll cure you of that silly notion." Gunner was determined to help.

It wouldn't be hard to cure him given he'd yet to meet a woman who intrigued him for more than one night. Usually by morning, he was ready to move on— and not leave a number.

He downed another shot of whiskey, savoring the fiery burn, and spreading languor in his limbs. Who needed a woman's soft embrace when he could drown himself in liquor?

"Speaking of pussy, did you have to kill Meathead?" Lash shook his head.

"No, I should have kept him alive so we could go for a beer. What the fuck do you think?" was his sarcastic reply.

Gunner shrugged. "Killing him might have created some complications."

"What kind of complications?" Gavin asked, signaling the barkeep for another shot.

"The guy was married," Gunner said while Lash made a moue.

"Not anymore he isn't." A smug smile tugged Gavin's lips.

"His wife is pissed."

"Again, not understanding why that's my problem." When men took chances, they sometimes paid the price.

Gunner felt a need to explain. "You killed her husband."

"Excuse me for not laying down to die."

"Couldn't you have just maimed him?" Gunner asked.

"Short of chopping off his arms and legs, would that have stopped him from coming after me?" Gavin asked, weary of it all, most especially this conversation. It didn't help he felt an odd twinge.

Guilt? Surely not. He did what he had to. If he'd not killed the beast, he would have died instead.

"True. The guy wasn't the type to take losing all that well. And apparently neither is his family."

"Meaning?"

"Rumor has it Meathead's wife and sons are coming after you." Gunner provided that little tidbit.

"To do what? Exact revenge?" Gavin's lips pulled into a smirk. "Do they want to join their daddy?"

Lash chuckled. "Oh, no dude. You misunderstand. They're not out to kill you. Apparently, since you took away their family breadwinner, they're going to marry you to one of the sisters."

"Excuse me? Like fuck am I marrying the beast's daughter."

"Better than the mother. That was the original plan, so I hear. But the sons kind of figured you'd balk, so they convinced mama dear to marry off their oldest sister," Gunner said.

"Still not fucking happening." Gavin tossed back another shot and then snared the bottle from the bartender before he could walk away with it. He chugged some of the liquid warmth.

But Gunner wasn't done. "You won't have a choice, dude. Word on the street is they're bringing a priest and muscle. Either you marry the girl, or you're toast."

The alcohol went down the wrong tube as shock made Gavin sputter. He slammed down the bottle on the counter as he coughed and hacked. His eyes watered. "Not getting married," he gasped between chokes.

"Are you sure? Because just a minute ago you were whining about how you thought one pussy for ever and ever was your new dream," Gunner mocked him.

"If I'm going to settle down, it will be with a woman *I* choose," Gavin growled.

"You know what they say about beggars," Lash sang.

"Except I'm not a beggar."

"You might be a dead man, though. Really, is it such a big deal? Marry the girl. Bang her a few times. Maybe plant a seed. And when she pulls her shrew shit, fuck off for a while. Bang a few ladies until she behaves again." Lash seemed to have all the answers.

Gavin tossed him a side eye. "Not only do you have me marrying a stranger, now you have me cheating on her? Doesn't that defeat the purpose of settling down with one woman?"

Lash shrugged. "Just trying to help you out."

"I've had enough of your help."

"So ungrateful," Gunner said with a shake of his head.

"I'd be more grateful if you'd not gotten me embroiled in this mess in the first place. This was supposed to be just a fight. Not the winner gets a shotgun wedding."

"If you're determined to stay single, then just leave." Lash offered the simplest solution.

One his battered body preferred to fighting it out. He shoved away from the bar. "Might as well. I've done my business here." He'd been done for a few days, actually. He just hadn't found the motivation to leave and start a new job.

"Leave before he's enjoyed the fruit of his spoils?" Gunner exclaimed, waggling his fingers at a bevy of woman batting their lashes at the other end of the bar.

Gavin tried to muster some enthusiasm, but truly, he was more interested in a soft pillow right now than the work involved in getting a woman off.

"If he doesn't want them, then we'll just have to be good friends and ensure we compensate them for their disappointment," Lash said.

"I guarantee no disappointment here." Gunner leered in their direction. "I've got plenty to satisfy."

"I've got more," Lash declared.

"In your dreams, stubby."

"Everyone knows a fat dick is better than long and lean."

"Says you," Gunner sneered. "Mine can reach those sweet spots."

"I reach just fine."

"Again, says you. I say we put our dicks to the test and let the orgasms scream for themselves."

"You're on." They slapped hands and Gavin shook his head.

The idiocy of the pair of them truly boggled the mind at times, and yet, they made him laugh. Probably why he'd not yet slit their throats and left them in an alley somewhere. They might not be the brightest friends, but despite all the trouble they got Gavin into, they had his back. And apparently would handle his winning pussy.

He clapped them both on the back. "While you guys enjoy your battle of the penis, I'm going to hit the sack. I want to be rested to go in the morning. My ship is fueled and stocked for my next voyage."

"You can't go to your ship yet." Lash shook his head. "We weren't kidding about that broad and her kids coming after you."

"Good thing I'm not going straight there then." Tired of his cramped cabin and foam mattress, Gavin had rented a room for his stay—under Cole's name. No use announcing his whereabouts.

The past few days he'd enjoyed the luxury of long hot showers, fresh food, and a soft mattress with fresh sheets.

I am getting so old.

"You're not hitting the Palm Tree resort, are you?" Gunner asked.

That surprised him. "How do you know about my room at the Palm Tree?"

"You didn't exactly expect us to leave you alone once we knew you docked."

"Did it occur to you that perhaps I wanted to be left alone?" That he didn't want to get involved in any bullshit.

"No."

Sigh. "So, is it safe to hit my room or not?" Should he book another place?

"We might have accidentally divulged your location." Lash whistled innocently as Gunner explained.

"I don't believe in accidents."

"It was an honest mistake," Gunner insisted.

"I doubt that. Who did you idiots tell?" Gavin asked, refraining from sighing.

"It wasn't the widow and her kids, if that's what you're wondering about," Gunner declared.

"We haven't talked to her at all. Yet," Lash added with a smile.

"Not entirely true, we did knock out that one guy and toss him in the drink."

Gavin sighed. "I'm afraid to ask why?"

"Because he spotted you coming into the bar."

"Everyone knows I'm in the bar. The fight was just outside."

"Yeah, but his job was to let Meathead's family know when you left and where you went. So we took care of him."

"Why does it feel like there's an 'and' to this conversation?"

"Because we didn't take him out quick enough. The widow is on her way with her sons."

Another sigh escaped him and Gavin pinched the bridge of his nose. "How long do I have before she arrives?" And why couldn't these morons tell him this before he got slightly drunk?

Peering at the door that led to the road, Gunner declared, "No time. I think that's Meatball's kid over there."

The hulking body and dumb expression sure resembled the one he'd fought in the ring. Great. The kids were beast-sized too.

Gavin slid off the stool. "I'm going to exit via the back."

Lash shook his head. "They've probably already got it covered. But don't worry, we thought this might be a problem, so Gunner has a plan."

"Does it involve killing you?" Gavin growled, his irritation simmering.

"Kill your bestest friends?" Gunner clasped his chest. "Dude, that is just rude."

"And funny. As if you could take us," Lash snickered.

"So, what's your plan then?" Judging by the glint in their eyes, he probably wouldn't like it, but if it got him out of here in one piece and without any new bruises, then it was worth it.

He'd need to be intact to strangle them both later.

"Just come with us to the bathroom for a minute and we'll show you," Gunner said.

The matching grins did nothing to reassure.

CHAPTER FIVE

WAITING AS DISCREETLY AS POSSIBLE IN THE SMALL restaurant across the street, Steph almost missed him when he emerged.

The Seadog fellow had chosen an unexpected guise. If it hadn't been for the pair of fellows flanking him, the same ones that she'd overheard with the clue to his whereabouts, she might have missed him.

And not because he blended in.

What the hell is he wearing?

Not much. Somehow, Gavin had gone from looking macho and dangerous to slinky and seductive.

In other words, he looked like a male whore. His jeans had been cropped short, showing off muscled thighs. His shirt had been ditched, displaying those impressive abs and thick arms. Silver rings pinched his nipples. His hair was spiked in a greasy mess. His lips were rouged and his eyes, rimmed in thick kohl, couldn't manage sultry. Was she the only one who noticed the dark and dangerous glint in them?

She understood the reason for the disguise. Several

strapping guys had entered the tavern, and—given their strong resemblance to Daddy—it wasn't hard to figure out why.

She was kind of surprised a guy like Gavin would stoop to hiding rather than battling it out; then again, Zola always taught her to fight smart, and bad odds called for retreat rather than brashness.

Brash fighters died young.

The keen gaze of a hunter, not a simpering prostitute, scanned the people in the street, still crowded even at this late evening hour. The night life tended to go until the wee hours of morning.

The big brutes lying in wait didn't pay Gavin and his forced pout any mind, their gaze bobbing between a phone someone held up and the door. Relying on a picture.

Idiots.

Steph stood from the table where she'd been nursing a cold drink and a roti—a delicious island pastry with spicy meat. The scrape of the chair shouldn't have been loud with the din in the place, and yet it drew his attention.

Cold eyes swept over her, caught her gaze for a moment, before dismissing her.

A typical man with a misogynistic attitude.

Having slipped past those searching for him, Gavin stalked through the crowd, completely ruining his disguise, and yet no one seemed to note the disparity of a whore strutting as if he owned the road.

And damned if he didn't get looks. Men and women alike stared, the hunger in some gazes irritating Steph.

Hands off. He's mine. But only if she could get to him.

A petite older woman had arrived, and began

berating the group by the tavern, jabbing a finger at them. It seemed the brains in that family belonged to the fairer sex because she'd no sooner finished her harangue than the brutes took off after Gavin.

The woman shouted, "Don't hurt him too much .We need him alive for your sister."

Steph's lips tightened in annoyance. Fuck this lady and her daughter. *I call dibs.* She had more need of him than they did.

Sweeping through the gawking crowd, because everyone loved to watch a fight, Steph made it to the rear of the giant boys going after Gavin.

She knew what Zola would say. *Head down. Don't get involved.* But this man might know something about Ronin.

If she wanted Gavin alive long enough to question then Steph should probably help even the odds.

Attack them without warning?

Zola taught her to not fight unless provoked.

Steph nudged against a fellow who didn't even look before shoving her hard.

I'd say that was provoking.

With only the slightest whisper of sound, hidden among the din, Steph slid her baton from her pocket and flicked it to extend it. Then she danced among the bodies, wielding it with painful precision.

Her teacher had taught Steph many tactics for fighting in a crowd. When more than one opponent faced you, you had to be efficient. There was no time for polite exchanges and by the book blows.

Every second, every motion counted.

Which meant she gave no warning, made no sound, as she incapacitated the much taller guys—a sharp blow to their knees sending them to the ground screaming. Her body weaved and spun as she wound through their ranks, felling at least three of them, leaving about five or so more. The blunt end of her baton cracked bones, bruised kidneys, and in general created chaos.

It served its purpose and distracted most of the thugs from their quarry. Even funnier, none of the big bullies suspected the petite woman ghosting among them as the one responsible for their pain.

As she bobbed amongst the confused attackers, she caught glimpses of her target. He'd opted for a knife, and the silver edge flashed.

Some might wonder at the fact no one pulled a gun. Perhaps in other places they would. In tourist towns, especially amongst crowds, even criminals knew to behave. Scare the tourists or draw too much attention and someone higher on the food chain would take exception at seeing their easy money dry up.

Break the rules and you might find yourself one of the bodies that floated ashore, hands severed, eyes plucked, and teeth smashed. Rival and petty squabbles were allowed, but only within certain bounds.

A strange code of ethics for unethical acts.

Gavin's companions didn't use blades, but relied on their fists to dispense violence. If she'd not already seen their Seadog friend in action, she might have admired them more. Their brute strength had its own kind of beauty, but lacked finesse.

The melee drew attention. Whistles blew as what passed for the local police arrived to join the fray, their batons uncaring of who they hit. Even women weren't exempt. A whack from behind had Steph snarling as she whirled. A grab and twist of the offending arm took care of that cop's baton whirling days.

One would have thought the cops arriving would disperse the fight, that the thugs would relinquish their attack, or that those watching would flee.

Instead, it acted as a magnet drawing more curious onlookers, more people to the brawl. Violence begat violence.

It didn't help that the older woman arrived, shouting loud encouragement. "Get him, babies. Get him for your mama."

What an annoying cunt.

Whirling, Steph pinpointed her in the crowd, noted the avarice shining her gaze. The woman, her dark hair streaked with gray and loose around her shoulders, practically foamed at the mouth in excitement.

With a flick of her wrist, Steph sent the baton she'd stolen from the cop flying. Her aim proved true as it hit the old lady in the noggin and knocked her out.

The melee was a mass of bodies gyrating and thrusting and screaming. Steph doubted anyone knew who they fought at this point, everyone just caved to the blood lust.

It took some maneuvering and a few broken bones to work her way to the spot she last saw her target.

Stomping on a guy's foot, then ramming her baton down on the hand that dared to grab her ass, she looked up from his sobs, and came face to face with Gavin.

His glacial eyes scrutinized her for a moment, a heart-stopping second during which everything else faded to nothing, nothing but the two of them.

She blinked, and the moment was shattered. He whirled away and dove through an opening, sprinting away from the mess, displaying a tight ass barely covered by his indecent shorts.

A good thing no one with any skill stood nearby because Steph gawked.

You idiot. He's getting away. Follow him.

Leaving the brawl behind, she sprinted after her target and noted him heading for the docks.

She pounded after him, but his head start and longer legs meant he left her behind.

Knowing she had no chance of capturing or even overpowering him, Steph veered instead for the berth assigned to her and Zola when they arrived.

Chances were he planned to set sail and it wouldn't do to lose him now. His sleek yacht was probably a lot more powerful than their little fishing vessel. But the man couldn't sail forever.

Out on the open ocean there would be less distraction. She could do whatever she liked to get the answers she needed.

And if he proved reluctant? Then good thing she'd brought along some rope.

CHAPTER SIX

BOARDING HIS BOAT, GAVIN FELT NO QUALMS ABOUT leaving Lash and Gunner behind. They knew how to acquit themselves, and seeing as how they were mostly to blame in the first place, it served them right.

Knowing those two idiots, they'd somehow come out ahead from the fight. He, on the other hand, now sported new bruises and a lost chance to get with the chick he'd come face to face with during the fight.

The redhead he'd exchanged a glance with during the ring fight was back, this time with a baton in hand and a savage light in her eyes.

Having spotted her during the battle, he wondered if she was a mercenary. She certainly fought like one.

She'd flowed through the ranks of Meatball's progeny like a deadly ghost, whacking with cool efficiency, but why? Why the interest in helping him?

It made no sense. Just like his sudden captivation with just a lock of gazes puzzled him.

What is it about her that is so intriguing? So deadly.

The brief moment they'd shared almost made him

forget the danger around him. Almost made him wish he had chosen a career as a pirate who dealt in flesh, then he might have tossed her over a shoulder and absconded with her.

But smart pirates didn't bring women on board. They were bad luck.

Just look at Cole. He'd dragged one onto his ship with his fish net and now was borderline hitched.

But Cole's abduction of Lillie was accidental whereas Gavin contemplated an intentional one because he was intrigued.

Don't be a moron. Forget the woman. Even he had more self-preservation than to knowingly kidnap a woman who A) showed an interest in him, and B) knew how to wield a stick.

I've got a stick she can play with.

Not exactly the most couth come-on line. And a moot point. He wouldn't be getting involved with the redhead. A man preferred not to sleep with one eye open, and to awake with his balls intact.

Speaking of balls, was her interest perhaps because they'd screwed in the past? Did she want a second go at him?

Gavin couldn't recall ever fucking her, then again, sometimes when the rum flowed copiously, he didn't remember his own name.

Why am I thinking about that chick when I should be setting sail?

He quickly undid the ropes mooring his boat to the dock. Unlike Cole with his big fishing vessel, Gavin opted for a sleeker yacht, one easily handled by a single man.

He threw the ropes onto the deck. He'd coil them

later. He braced his foot against the dock and shoved, the buoyant seawater easing the passage of his boat. He darted to the wheelhouse and started his engine, the soft purr making the deck underfoot hum.

Given the many lights illuminating the other ships, he didn't bother switching his on, the better to slip away in darkness.

His bigger dilemma was where to go. Still in between jobs, he was too restless to go stay a stint at his home, but he was also too weary to go looking for trouble.

He propped his smartphone on his dash and addressed it. "Yo, babe, is there anywhere I can go where I have no enemies or bounties on my head?" he grumbled aloud as he navigated the crowded waters of the bay.

He received a soft, machine quality reply. "Sorry, but I don't understand that question."

"Or course you don't," he mumbled. "Any messages?"

"Negative."

Nobody needed him. Nobody wanted him.

Shoot me now for sounding like a big fucking pussy.

Perhaps he should have stuck around the port; at least he was wanted there.

And that intriguing redhead was there, too.

Much as it pained to admit, Gavin needed to lay low for a while, lick his wounds. The smart thing was head home. Home all alone. How boring.

Fuck that. "Yo, babe, what do you say we go visit my ol' buddy Cole?"

"Sorry, I don't understand that question.

"It's called cock blocking, babe. If I can't find a

woman to be happy with, then goddammit, no one should." Perhaps while he was there, he'd figure out why he envied Cole, or cure himself of it.

Funny how a few weeks ago he'd scoffed at Cole for pretty much retiring from smuggling to become a cog in the business with a home office and occasional visits into the mainland to meet face to face with the boss.

Now, Gavin found himself envious. In all the years he'd known Cole, he'd never seem him so content. So…happy.

Quite honestly, Gavin didn't understand it. But he coveted it. Could he find the same?

Let a woman shackle me? Don't you remember how that worked last time?

He knew all too well how duplicitous women could be. They only used men to get what they wanted, be it riches, power, or vengeance. Give a woman what she asked for and next thing a guy knew, she showed her true colors and fucked him over.

Right, Bella? You fooled me with your innocent eyes and lies. He wouldn't fall for that again. Not ever.

Forget settling down. Women served only one purpose in his life—pleasuring him. And even if they did it well, he rarely went back for seconds. Why bother when he always had someone new and willing to climb atop his dick for a spin?

What about when I'm older, will I still be able to attract pussy? Even if he got grizzled, or fat—like fuck—he'd always be able to rent someone for an hour or two.

Which is pathetic. Loser, I can't even believe—

Beep. Beep.

The radar showed a blip, not unusual given he still

sailed close to the island of Jamaica. But, given most people set sail in the morning or during daylight hours, it was a touch unusual.

Gavin was suspicious by nature, which was why he had yet to activate his onboard lights. It went against a whole bunch of international maritime regulations, but he didn't give a flying fuck. Darkness was his friend and his cloak.

The blip on his screen faded away, and he relaxed. Just a coincidence.

A few hours out from port, he dropped anchor and finally turned on some lights. The radar still swept, showing nothing, and synced with his smartphone. He set it to notify him if anything changed.

Heading below, Gavin took a second to strip out of the uncomfortable shorts. Booty shorts, a thing no man should ever wear.

He also took a moment to scrub his face and stick his head under water to clean the gunk from his hair. The disguise was a good one. Most people didn't give the boytoys on the island a second glance unless they were looking for action. But Gavin was no one's toy.

Although, I might make an exception for Red.

Argh. What the fuck was with his obsession over a woman he'd seen twice? A woman he'd never see again.

He did not feel depressed at the thought. Just tired.

He checked his radar link to his ship. Still nothing on the screen. A clean getaway.

Fatigue pulling at him, he dropped into his bunk. He quickly fell asleep only to find himself woken much too soon by the jarring sound of an alarm.

Someone or something is too close.

He no sooner sat up when something rocked his ship.

Big fish? Could be. These waters played host to all kinds of species, including great whites and whales. But he was in fairly shallow waters, and his alarm scanned for things above, not below the surface.

So what did that leave?

Thump. The distinct sound of someone landing on his deck.

I'm being boarded.

Some asshole was about to learn what a bad idea that was. But before he could grab his gun, or at least throw on some shorts, the cabin filled with smoke.

CHAPTER SEVEN

STAYING OUT OF RADAR SIGHT OF GAVIN'S CRAFT proved easy, especially since Zola had planted a bug on his hull.

"You did what?" Steph asked once she boarded the ship.

"I had a few left over from a job, so I took a swim—"

"In the dirty port waters?" Steph wrinkled her nose.

"I borrowed a shower from a friend."

"That was risky," Steph said. "I thought we were supposed to stay low."

"Says the girl who got involved in a brawl."

"I didn't start it," was her indignant reply.

"Hmph."

"So where is he heading?"

Zola shrugged as she guided their small ship. "No idea, but we'd better catch him quick because that tracking device won't last long in these waters."

Until the battering ocean waves killed the electronic device, it would emit a very low signal pulse that they could follow. Keeping a close eye on it meant they noticed when he stopped moving.

"He's dropped anchor for the night," Zola observed. "We'll go in on silent wings."

By wings she meant using their sails for stealth. But even then they had to go in fast because they couldn't foil his radar. While there were tools for knocking those devices offline, they were pricey and unwanted weight on a small ship.

As the pulse of the tracker got closer, Steph couldn't help a spurt of excitement. Almost within reach of her quarry. Soon she'd get some answers about her brother —and come face to face once again with *him*.

The thought made her shiver.

They sailed ever closer, making straight for his location. Ever impatient, Steph made her way to the edge of the ship, clutching the railing, so that when the sailboat veered at the last moment and almost bumped his, she was close enough to simply toss the gas canister into the dark hole of his hatch.

The gas would take a moment to render him unconscious, but she still hurried to don her mask to protect her from fumes before she leaped from her ship to his.

The deck lights provided spots of illumination through the wisping smoke. Given he didn't have a huge ship, she only spent a moment scanning the smoky deck before turning her attention to the wheelhouse. Was he up there or down below? The smoke would have infiltrated both areas.

Pulling out the gun she'd slipped into her waistband, she first clambered up the few steps to peek inside, heart hammering, hands clutching the grip damply.

Empty.

She heaved a shuddering breath.

She'd not been this nervous during the fight, and yet now, moments from encountering him, a strange anxiousness invaded her.

Had the gas worked, or would she run into a very pissed off man? If she did, a bullet would stop him dead —*but I don't want him dead.*

Not until she got what she needed from him.

Slowly, she inched down the stairs to the cabin below. The mask muffled her senses, making each breath sound inordinately loud. Did he hear her? Did the racing of her heart give her away?

A part of her wished Zola was beside her, there to help her if needed, but her teacher had remained on their boat stating, "Don't be a chicken shit. You got this. Remember what I taught you."

Steph remembered. The problem was when she'd practiced with Zola, she knew she might get hurt, but nothing fatal would happen.

Now…uncertainty twisted her gut.

Was this how Ronin felt when he went on a mission? Or did this gut churning trepidation fade the more times he went out?

Thinking of her brother strengthened her. She was doing this for him.

Deep breath in and out—which made her sound like Darth Vader—and another step brought her into the bowel of the ship. Darkness reigned, everything powered down to preserve the onboard batteries. A sleek and small vessel like this would rely mostly on solar when not in motion so as to preserve fuel.

A standard yacht, she kind of knew the layout. A fumble to her side brought her fingers in contact with a switch and she flicked it, the light illuminating the space dim, but still bright enough to make her blink.

Almost instantly she heard Zola chiding in her head, "Stupid. You just gave away your position."

It could have cost her life, if her target weren't snoring in a heap on the floor. The gas had knocked him out.

You're mine now. The words aroused a strange satisfaction.

Kneeling by his side, she rolled him onto his back, not easily. The man was freaking huge. But once she got him partway up, gravity helped and he flopped over.

She took a moment to study him. It seemed a shame to ignore his handsome features. His rugged features, she should add, given only his lips appeared full and soft. Everything else, from his square chin to his jagged nose —broken one too many times to heal straight—to the five o-clock shadow on his cheeks, screamed *I am man.*

And sexy. She might not be very experienced with the opposite sex, but as a woman, she noticed, and liked.

A glance at his body, his very nude body, showed the musculature she'd admired before. Even better, she knew it wasn't for show. He knew how to move and use that strength.

He had a light dusting of hair on his chest, not a man who shaved it. In the islands, it was common to have it removed, but he'd opted to leave it. That hair spread down his torso, narrowing into a vee that led to thicker curls and a limp cock.

It looked so defenseless, nothing like the mighty sword men were always bragging about.

But that's only because he's asleep. Her education had taught her—as had the videos she'd watched with wide eyes behind her closed bedroom door—just how big a penis could get, especially if stroked right.

But I won't be touching his cock.

Then why was she still staring at it?

She gave herself a shake. Get with the program. She wasn't here to have fun or lose her cherry. She had a job to do, a brother to save, and this man had the answers she needed.

Given the drug wouldn't last forever, she had to get him in position before he woke. Except that proved easier planned than done. He weighed a freaking ton. When she tried to lift him, she only managed to get him inches off the floor, and when she tried to pull him, he didn't budge!

Dammit.

With a heavy thump and her chest heaving, she dropped him. Now what? Her plan didn't involve her questioning him on the floor while she stood over him. Then again…the things she could do to him were tantalizing.

No. Stop it. She needed to stick with the game plan and not veer into weird nympho territory.

Explain that to her body that suddenly decided to rebel against her virgin state, not a state she chose by choice. Her brother threatened to kill anyone who went near her. Add in Zola who just promised castration and it was no wonder Steph remained untouched.

But not for lack of wanting. Having Gavin at her mercy, remembering his body as it gleamed during the fight, arousal exploded.

Now is not the time.

She planted her hands on her hips and glared at him. This was his fault.

Stomping back up the steps, she ripped off the mask and bellowed, "I need a hand."

Zola, who'd dropped anchor and sat dangling her feet in the water, clapped.

Steph glared. "This isn't funny. I can't move him. He's too bloody big."

"Where is he? On the throne taking a shit?"

Her cheeks turned hot. "No. He passed out on the floor."

"And?"

"I need him on a chair, or at least in bed."

"You need to get moving before he wakes up and decides to wring your neck. I've heard things about this Crusty Seadog person. He's not a man who takes slights to his person lightly."

"Then stop yapping and help me."

With a huge sigh, Zola heaved herself to her feet. "The things I do for you."

"Oh, please. You're about to thank me because did I mention he's stark freaking naked?"

At that, Zola's expression brightened and she hastened her step. Steph's teacher might be pushing her forties, but her appetite for the opposite sex was strong.

Skipping down the steps, Zola emitted a low whistle. "Well hello there, big boy."

Steph shoved past her teacher. "Don't just stand staring. We need to move him."

"We could just tie him up here and have our way with him." Zola licked her lips.

"What do you mean have our way?" Steph paused in her grabbing of his arms to gape at Zola.

"You're not that innocent, dawta."

"We are not here to have fun," she snapped. Oddly, it wasn't the suggestion itself that bothered her, that heated her blood. What she didn't like was Zola's suggestion she'd be touching him, too.

"Get out of my way. I got this." Zola had experience with heavy, passed out men. It happened all the time at the compound when the boys got old enough to test their drinking limits. In mere moments, Zola had him draped over her shoulders. She stood with a grunt. "He's got some weight to him."

Good thing they didn't have far to go.

Zola heaved him onto the bunk and then stood back.

"Now what? He's going to wake soon."

"Go back to our ship. I got this," Steph said. She had an idea. She got to work with her portable drill—Zola never left the compound without some basic tools—and bolted some rings into the bed frame and the wall. Then, she threaded some rope through them. She quickly tied his arms and legs, stretching the limbs of his powerful body, unable to avoid his heated skin against her own as she clambered over him to make the knots secure.

The contact did strange things to her body. Made her shiver. Her breasts ached. Even her pussy got in on the act, wetting her panties.

Despite knowing he was her enemy, she couldn't resist stroking a hand down his muscled chest. But no further than that. She avoided looking at his cock.

Avoided looking and yet she didn't cover it.

Eventually, she was done securing him and just in time too.

He stirred, his head moving slightly, his eyelids

twitching. She hurried to turn off the light to retain the element of surprise.

Let the torture for answers begin.

____

CHAPTER EIGHT

____

His head pounded.

His mouth was dry.

His lids unbearably heavy.

Felt like a hangover, except he wasn't drunk when he went to sleep.

So why do I feel like shit?

He groaned and went to roll over, only his body didn't move. What the fuck?

Opening his eyes, he frowned because he was obviously on his ship and in his bed. Despite the dimness, he recognized the ceiling, except why did he have a recollection of getting out of bed?

There was an alarm, and then a bump.

Then smoke.

But his ship obviously hadn't burned down and he'd not become a barbecued version of himself. So, exactly what happened?

Don't be a moron. You know what happened. Someone gassed him. But who? And why the fuck was he tied to his goddamned bed?

Not just tied, spread eagle and buck naked.

His first impulse was to squeeze his ass cheeks, checking for signs of soreness of abuse.

His sphincter felt fine, so nobody had shoved anything in his out hole yet, but finding himself bound and naked didn't bode well.

It meant whoever got the drop on him wanted him awake for whatever perversion they had planned.

I don't suppose I could hope for a hot and bored debutante looking to piss off her daddy by fucking a mercenary.

That only happened in *Seducing her Semen*, volumes one through fourteen. In real life, those doing the seducing were smelly and bearded.

I am not about to become some dirty pirate's glory hole.

Yanking first with his arms and then his legs, Gavin scowled. Someone had tied him rather securely. Even more insulting, they'd used his rope and not left him any slack to work with.

"I am going to kill someone," he muttered.

"Might be kind of hard given your position." A light flicked on and he blinked as a woman came into view.

"You." Said flatly—mostly to hide his excitement. He recognized that red hair.

Her head tilted to the side. "You know who I am?"

"No. But I saw you. Back on the islands. What do you want?"

"I need something from you."

"You could have just asked." He wiggled his hips and, despite the situation, his cock stirred.

To his shock—and a bit of intrigued delight—her cheeks turned a bright shade of pink.

"I didn't tie you up for *that*." Spoken with emphasis and even brighter cheeks.

"Are you sure?" He waggled his hips again, the stir of his cock, rising from its nest, drawing her attention.

Her eyes widened. "Stop that."

"Why? You obviously kidnapped me for a reason. And since you tied me to a bed naked, it doesn't take a genius to figure it out."

"I didn't—that is—" She appeared flustered, which was kind of cute. Or would have been if the roles were reversed. Being tied up wasn't his idea of a good time.

I like to be in control.

But if he had to be anyone's captive, she made a good choice. He gave her a long look, one that started from the top of her head, crowned in that reddish blonde mane, pulled back from her face. Her face appeared as fine as porcelain with a light pattern of freckles across the bridge of her nose and cheeks.

She wasn't tall. Even if he'd not seen her in person while upright, he'd have guessed that given how she stood beside his bed and yet would need a boost to get on it. He'd opted for a captain's bunk with storage underneath.

She might be petite in stature, but she was blessed with a sweet pair of tits. The heavy handfuls rounded the fabric of her t-shirt. The nipples protruded slightly despite her bra and the more he stared, the more pronounced they became. Veritable hard nubs poking and demanding attention.

He might have licked his lips and said, "Yummy."

Arms whipped over the tempting buds. "Ahem." She intentionally cleared her voice.

He raised his gaze to meet her green-eyed one. His lips pulled into a lopsided smile. "Just admiring the goods, Ariel."

"That's not my name."

"Because you never gave me one, but given you're a red-headed temptress at sea, I'd say it fits."

"I'm not a mermaid."

"Obviously. No tail. Or is it hiding under those shorts?" He deliberately checked out her lean legs. "I don't see any scales. Why don't you drop those pants and let me check your ass."

"Stop it."

"Stop what? Admiring your assets? What else would you like me to do? I am, after all, tied up. At your mercy. Be gentle."

At those words, her expression tightened. "This isn't funny. I need you to take me seriously."

"Oh, but I do, Ariel. So seriously that when I get loose, I'm going to wring your little neck before tossing you overboard."

"You won't get loose."

"You'd better hope I don't or you're going to be on your knees begging, with your mouth around my cock for clemency. I'm not a man who forgives easily, but if you blow me just right..." He winked. "Maybe you can suck your way to forgiveness."

The crude words had the desired effect. Her cheeks once again bloomed with color.

"This isn't about sex."

"Then what is this about, Ariel? Because before last night, we'd never met." He would have remembered her. "So why have you attacked me?"

"I didn't attack you. Exactly."

"Am I not tied to my bed?"

"Yes, but I haven't hurt you. Yet." She tried for an ominous tone.

It was cute. He armored himself against it. "Hurt me and your punishment will be worse."

"Maybe you're the one who should be worried I'm going to hurt you."

"You, hurt me?" He couldn't help the rich laughter, and it only increased in timbre the more she scowled.

"I will hurt you if you don't give me the answers I need."

"Go ahead. Do your worst." A deliberate taunt, and possibly a dumb one given he'd seen her in action. Still, she had some kind of use for him, so he trusted that would keep him safe until he extricated himself.

"Aren't you going to ask me what I want to know?"

"Nope. Because I'm not a snitch, so whatever information you're looking for is too bad so sad. I ain't telling you."

Her lips pursed. "Oh yes you will."

"No, I won't." He meant what he said. Gavin would never spill the beans on anyone, not by force. Now, if she'd asked him nicely… Nah. Even then, he wasn't one to cough up info on the people he knew.

She held up a fist. "Tell me where my brother is."

"Even if I knew who the fuck you were talking about, I wouldn't. If your brother wanted his nosy sister to know, he'd tell you."

She slugged him. A tiny fist with great form, but not enough weight behind it. "Tell me."

"No."

She hit him again, and again.

He laughed. "Oh that tickles. Do it lower, would you. My thighs could use a massage."

With a growl of frustration, she shoved away from him. "Why can't you just tell me where my brother is?"

He was curious as to why she thought he knew. She'd not even told him her brother's name, yet she expected him to have information. The girl might have some fighting skills, but she obviously lacked common sense.

"Did it ever occur to you to ask instead of abducting me?"

She whirled. "If I promised to let you go, would you tell me?"

"No."

"You're a fucking asshole."

"So people tell me."

That earned him an inarticulate sound of rage. Did she even know how cute she looked when she was pissed?

"This doesn't have to get ugly, if you'll just talk to me." She growled, the words meant to be low and menacing. He deciphered them more as low and sexy.

"How about you talk to my dick? He likes oral conversation." He arched a brow and restrained a laugh as she turned pink and speechless.

But he made a mistake speaking about his cock. She hit him.

In the sac.

That made him oomph. "Bitch."

"Does that hurt?" She grabbed hold of his throbbing balls and squeezed. "Tell me where my brother is." She leaned over him, her face so close he could almost touch those hissing lips.

"You want to know so bad, why don't you fix what you just tried to break."

"Excuse me?" Such a polite exclamation from his captor.

"I said, why don't you climb on top of my dick for a spin and then we'll talk."

"I am not having sex with you."

"Your loss." It surprised Gavin to note despite the situation, and her grievous blows to his balls, he couldn't help a surge of lust when she licked her lips.

Those lips were perfectly curved and full and would look so much better wrapped around his cock rather than nagging him about some bloke he'd never met. The things he could do to that delectable mouth. He could so easily picture grabbing her by that fiery colored ponytail and holding her in place as he thrust into her mouth.

Hadn't anyone ever taught her to use her wiles to get what she wanted? But no, she just had to do something foolish like take him prisoner. Perhaps had she tried getting on her knees first, he might have at least told her he didn't know shit after she blew him.

Just thinking about her touching his dick made it rise and she took notice.

No surprise her cheeks went pink and her eyes widened. She played the innocent so well. Good thing he saw through the act.

"No need to stare, Ariel. It's okay if you want to kiss it better."

She flashed him a glance. "If…" She swallowed hard —instead of spitting, good girl. "If I pleasured you, would it make a difference?"

"Why not touch me and see?" he said.

She approached him and stood hesitantly by the bed.

"What do you want me to do?"

She was good. He almost believed she'd never played with a cock before. "What do you want to do?"

She didn't reply, instead ran a finger, the nail on it squared and blunt, not a speck of polish on it down his chest.

Despite being a man of experience, a tremble went through him. Had it been so long since he'd fucked someone that just a simple touch wrought such a response?

The finger hesitated at the top of his pubes. His cock, on the other hand, strained from the nest of curls. It waved for her attention.

"I shouldn't be doing this." She muttered the words and he had to wonder if she realized she said them out loud.

More of her tricks?

Abruptly, she grabbed hold of him, wrapping her fingers around his length, a firm grip that had him sucking in a breath, his hips arching.

"Like this?" Slowly, she stroked him, her sensual slide of her hand at odds with the seeming innocence of her words.

Oh you are really good, Ariel.

So good he wanted to tilt his head back and close his eyes. But then that would mean he couldn't watch her. Couldn't see the curious tilt of her head as she observed her own hand stroking.

Did it excite her? It sure as fuck excited him.

"Untie me." The words emerged from him more roughly than expected.

The stroking of his cock halted, and her gaze flicked to meet his. "I don't trust you."

"Even if I promised to give you great pleasure?"

"You also promised to wring my neck when you got loose."

"That was before we came to an understanding. This doesn't have to be one-sided."

"What if I like you where you are?"

"I could do so much more if you released me."

"Zola says astride is the best position for a woman."

"Who is Zola?" he asked, only to hiss in surprise as she clambered onto the bed and straddled him.

"What are you doing?"

"Reminding you who's in charge here." She leaned forward, her lips but a hairsbreadth from his. "Don't think I don't know what you're doing."

"What am I doing, Ariel?"

"You're trying to seduce me."

"I'd do a better job with my hands free."

"You don't need your hands for me to ride you."

She sat squarely on his cock. Her shorts provided a barrier, and yet he still felt the heat of her, and dare he guess, moisture too?

"You're playing with fire."

"I am doing what I have to. This would be a lot easier if you'd cooperate."

"And I already told you I wouldn't tell you shit. So, why not spare us both the trouble and stop trying." What he didn't mention was it was too late for her to avoid punishment. The little cock tease would get what she had coming to her.

When I get loose, I'm going to bend you over my lap and spank that ass of yours.

And then he'd flip her over and fuck her hard.

"I can't stop. My brother needs me. Which means you have to tell me what you know."

"What makes you think I even know him?"

"I heard your name in the right. Your name is the only one I heard mentioned in conjunction with my brother. You were the last person to see him."

"I see lots of people."

"You'd remember my brother."

"Doesn't matter if I do. I ain't telling you shit." More because he was being obstinate. The woman wasn't pumping him for information on his boss or a job, just her poor sibling.

What if she lied, though? What if she wasn't this guy's sister at all? Women would do or say anything.

She dug her thumbs into his ribs, the tips of her fingers biting. "Tell me!"

"No."

The more times he said it, the redder her face turned. Of more interest were her odd ideas when it came to torture. She still sat astride, her crotch pressing against his rigid cock, her weight nothing but a tease. She switched from digging her fingers in to twisting his nipples.

That got him yelling. "Ow. What the fuck? This isn't grade school."

She twisted harder. "Talk."

"You can nurple me until they're purple. I ain't saying shit."

She yelled at him and pounded at his chest. Frustration boiled over and her face turned red as she whaled away at his body. "Rotten fucking jerk. Why won't you tell me? What have you done to him? Why? Why!" she screamed.

Only to suddenly stop and sit atop him, her chest heaving.

No hands to throttle her with meant he didn't have much recourse other than his mouth to fight back. So he did the only thing he could.

Closed his eyes and ignored her. Ignored her as she harangued him some more.

With a sound of annoyance, she climbed off him and left.

But he had no doubt she'd be back.

CHAPTER NINE

"WHAT AN ASSHOLE," STEPH MUTTERED AS SHE exited the cabin onto the main deck.

He heard her and hollered, "You're welcome."

She didn't dignify it with a reply. Then again, what dignity did she have left after her tantrum?

I lost control.

She wiped the hot tears on her cheek with the hem of her shirt, but it did nothing for her frustration.

"Why is he being so fucking stubborn?" She asked the question aloud and got a reply.

"Because he's a man."

She glared over the deck to see Zola had resumed her spot with feet dangling in the water. The tip of a cigarette glowed as her teacher took a drag.

"I thought you were supposed to quit smoking."

"A person's gotta have at least one vice."

"I thought your vices were drinking too much and one-night-stands."

White teeth gleamed in the dark. "Booty calls don't count because they're fun."

"Are you saying you don't enjoy smoking?"

The red tip of the cigarette flared bright for a moment as Zola drew hard on the cancer stick. Steph heard her breathing the smoke out as she said, "Hate it. Nasty stuff. Stinks to holy heaven. But fuck me if it's not the one thing that relaxes me."

"So does weed, and you can eat that instead of polluting the air."

Zola chuckled. "Yeah, but weed slows me down. And I can't afford to be sluggish outside the compound."

"Because everyone is your enemy, sometimes even those you think are friends," Steph recited by rote. Paranoia could be taught.

"Never forget it, dawta."

"But you trust me, and Ronin, and the other boys at the compound."

"You're my family. That's different."

Ignoring the fact she had a man tied up below, Steph took a seat at the rail and hugged it as she dangled her legs through the opening. "Zola, why didn't you ever settle down? You know, get married, have kids?"

"Why would you be asking me something like that?"

"Curiosity."

"Strange question to be asking now, don't you think? Is there something you're not telling me? Do you have a guy you're crushing on? Who is it? Malcolm?" An orphan like Steph, Malcolm was short and hairy.

She made a face.

"Kalvin?" Tall and reed thin, with a high-pitched voice and body odor issues.

Steph shuddered.

"Please don't tell me it's that womanizer Adam. I'll

tear off his balls and shove them down his throat if he's laid a hand on you."

A smile tugging her lips, Steph shook her head. "No. I'm not interested in anyone. Those guys are like brothers to me." Brothers for the younger ones, uncles for the older. Given the rules governing life amidst the gang, they treated her with kid gloves. No one wanted to deal with Zola or Ronin.

"So you're just curious like a cat. Careful it doesn't get you eaten."

"I'm always careful and you're avoiding the question," Steph pointed out.

Zola grimaced, the shadows not completely hiding a certain resignation in her gaze. "Since you insist on being a bug, I was in love once, a long time ago. This was back before I joined the gang, back when I lived on the main islands."

"What happened?"

The other woman's shoulders lifted and fell. "What always happens with a brash young man looking to score and make his mark. He took on something bigger than him. And failed."

"He died?"

"Yes. But he shouldn't have. If he'd had the right people to help him, if he would have let me help him, then things might have turned out different."

"Is that why you learned to fight?"

"I always knew how to fight." Teeth flashed. "But that is when I became more serious about it. I got into a lot of trouble after Danny died. Tried to fight away the pain of losing him. I caught the eye of Jerome, Henderson's recruiter. He approached me about becoming part of the gang, and after I stopped telling him to go fuck himself, I joined. Learned a fuck ton of stuff. I became the best merc they had."

Steph had heard the stories. In her day, Zola was quite the looker, which meant she could get into places the guys couldn't. Score jobs the others couldn't touch.

Older now and thicker, she opted to stay at the compound rather than in the field, teaching the recruits.

"Did you never love again?"

"I never allowed myself to. Losing Danny hurt. And I swore I'd never let it happen again."

"Is that why you won't let me date anyone in the gang?"

Zola snorted. "No. I don't let you date them because none of them are good enough for you. I want you to find love one day with a man worthy of you. Someone with a life outside the compound. You deserve kids, a family. You can't have that if you stay there."

"But if I left, I wouldn't have you."

Zola cast her a side eye. "As if you'd lose me so easily. I expect you to have a room reserved for whenever I choose to drop in."

"I'd first need to find a man for that."

"You have one down below."

"Gavin?" She exclaimed his name, her cheeks heating as she wondered if Zola had glimpsed her strange erotic interest in the man. "I wouldn't exactly call him boyfriend material."

"Why not?"

"You heard what our informant said. He's scum." According to the guy she'd wheedled the information from, Crusty Seadog was a down and dirty player who killed without cause, stole without contract, and was just an all-around shit.

A good-looking shit. But appearance didn't change what he was.

"There are some who would say our gang ain't much better."

Steph slashed a hand through the air. "Still not gonna happen. He wants to kill me for capturing him."

"So, you soften him up. Explain you did this for your brother. He'll understand."

"I doubt that."

"That's only because you haven't plied your feminine wiles on him."

"I wouldn't know how."

"It's not that hard. He's an attractive man. I'm sure you can think of things you'd like to do to him."

The problem was she could too easily picture all kinds of stuff. Even just the thought of touching him again lit a fire in her veins.

"I am not having sex with our prisoner. And I doubt he'll want to once I'm done with him. He won't answer my questions." Her lips turned down. "I'm going to have to get medieval with his ass."

Zola snorted. "Do you really think you can intentionally hurt the man?"

"I know how to hurt."

"Never said you didn't, but hurting someone in battle is a lot different from beating on someone who's tied up."

"What else am I supposed to do?" she asked. "I need to find out what he knows about Ronin and he won't answer me."

"And you think a man like that will respond to torture?" Zola shook her head, her dark locks flying. "I'd try something different."

"Like what?"

"Seduction."

Steph blinked. Wiggled a finger in her ear and said, "What the fuck did you just say?"

"I said, seduce the guy. Give him a blowjob. Or ride him like a cowgirl. Get him to pop his top."

"You want me to have sex with him?" She scrambled to her feet as she screeched it. "Are you nuts? What happened to no man being good enough for me?"

"No man in the gang is good enough for you. I told you, I want better for you."

"So you think I should throw myself at a stranger."

"I think you should experiment with a no strings hunk."

"No!"

"Why not?"

Because she didn't love him. Because sex for answers was wrong—at least the books she read said so. Because her brother would lose his mind. And then the more embarrassing part, what if she really liked it and he didn't? What if she sucked at seduction?

"It won't work," was the reply she settled on.

"You haven't even tried."

"And I won't, because it's crazy."

Zola shrugged as she lit another cigarette. "Says you. I'm going to speak from experience when I say I've gotten some of my best tidbits in the sack."

"But I'm a virgin."

"Gotta pop that cherry sometime. And quite honestly, it's best you do it with a stranger. The first poke sucks. And hurts. You can forget all those love stories that make it sound grand and majestic. It's not. It's painful and messy. Best to get it over with and move on so that when you meet the right one, you don't have it in the way."

Incredulity had Steph blurting, "I can't believe after all these years you're advocating I whore myself."

"You're not doing it for money."

"But I am doing it for answers, isn't that the same?"

"Do you want to find Ronin or not?"

"You know I do."

"Then shut up and do what you have to."

"Don't you mean do him?" she said sarcastically. "Speaking of whom, I should check on him. He's probably had enough time to think about how screwed he is." Maybe he'd be more amenable to talking.

Except when she popped down below it was to discover he'd undone the intricate knot on one hand and now worked on the other.

With a curse, she dashed to the bed just as he finished unknotting it.

Good news, his legs remained caught so he couldn't exactly leap off the bed. He wanted to, she could tell by his thunderous expression. Arms loose, though, meant he could sit up, and he did with a flex of his abs.

He crossed his arms over his chest and a wicked smile pulled his lips. "There's you are, Ariel. A moment too soon. A few more minutes and I could have greeted you properly."

Judging by his tone and expression, his greeting might have involved throttling.

"You won't escape."

"I'd say I'm halfway there. If I were you, I'd run now. Leave, and maybe, just maybe, I won't feel a need to punish you."

Cowering wouldn't serve any purpose, and Steph

knew from growing up with men that only brashness would earn her any kind of respect. "You haven't gotten out of that bed yet. And you can forget me going anywhere. I am not done with you."

"You're right, Ariel, we aren't done with each other." Said in a low, ominous tone.

"Stop calling me Ariel."

"Why not? You still haven't given me your name. Mine, by the way, is Gavin."

"I know. They announced it at the fight."

"Remember it because you're going to scream it when I get my hands on you."

She pursed her lips and tucked in her arms. "Ooh, I'm shaking in my knickers."

"I'd rather see you out of those knickers." His gaze dropped and she couldn't help a spurt of heat.

"You want me to undress for you?" She slid her hand to the button on her shorts. Slipped it from the loop. His gaze remained riveted as her fingers tugged at the zipper. "Exactly what would you do if I stripped?" she whispered huskily, sidling closer, getting near enough for him to grab, but hoping he stayed distracted.

"I would lick you until you screamed my name."

Shudder worthy words. But she fought past them, drew forth the syringe she'd stashed in her back pocket, and stabbed him with it.

He managed to utter a "Bitch!" and grab at her. No surprise his hands went for her throat, the fingers squeezing. Steph clawed at his grip, unable to call for help. Unable to draw a breath.

I'm going to die. He was going to choke her to death. She'd not been clever enough or fast enough.

Spots danced in front of her eyes as her lungs

screamed for air. Then his eyes, those blazing blue eyes, fluttered shut. His grip loosened and she managed to draw in a ragged breath. Then another.

That was close. Too close. But at least the sedative she'd thought to pack in her back pocket worked, but for how long?

Stop fucking around. She might not have much time. He'd slumped back onto the bed. Leaning over him, she grabbed the loose rope and quickly retied it. She knew she'd need more than rope this time. He'd already escaped them once.

Heading out to the deck, she leaped over the rail on to their ship and rummaged through their storage.

A curious Zola had followed her and asked, "Whatcha looking for?"

"Something sturdier than rope to hold him. He almost got away," she said, her voice a husky rasp.

"There's zip ties in the fishing box."

The long plastic binders would do the trick. Returning to his cabin, she pulled his arms over his head and lashed his wrists together.

Try getting loose now.

She stood back and surveyed her work, which meant she got a good look at him.

A sheen of sweat covered him. He'd obviously strained getting free. For some reason, her finger trailed a path down his chest, making its way to that defined vee.

Was Zola right? Would seduction be a better course than torture?

At rest, his cock didn't seem so fearsome, but she remembered its size from before. *No way am I losing my virginity to that monster-sized dick.*

She might be traumatized from sex for life.

"If you want sleeping dick to wake up, give it a kiss," he said in a husky murmur, startling her.

He'd recovered too damned fast. The dosage in her needle obviously wasn't enough for a man his size.

She shot him a sly look. "You'd like that, wouldn't you?"

"What man wouldn't want a gorgeous woman's lips on his dick?"

A part of her understood he played her, and yet, that didn't stop the spurt of pleasure. "What makes you think I want to kiss you?"

"I saw how you were staring."

She couldn't help but stare because he fascinated her. And damn him, if she wasn't curious. Who would it hurt? No one would know. And maybe Zola was right, maybe the soft approach would bear fruit.

Wrapping her hand around his firm cock, she bent over, pressed her lips against it, and made a noisy *muah* sound.

He snorted. "That was not a kiss."

"It involved lips," she said, turning sideways to speak to him, still holding on to his cock.

"A real kiss has tongue," he taunted.

"Apparently your dick doesn't need a lick." She inclined her head. "It's already woken up."

"All the more reason to keep going."

"You're something else."

"I'm like no one you'll ever meet, Ariel."

He had that right. Her soft chuckle blew hot air across the head of his shaft.

His body twitched and the dick in her grip hardened. This was probably a good time to step away. She'd satisfied some of her curiosity.

But not all of it.

How does he taste? Sticking out the tip of her tongue, she ran it across the swollen head. Salty.

She took another lick and while he said not a word, his breathing quickened.

Apparently, I'm doing something right. Which emboldened her to keep going. She blew on the skin she'd moistened. He definitely shuddered.

She popped the tip in to her mouth and sucked, getting more of that salty flavor. There was a certain powerful feeling having him at her mercy. To see and feel him responding to her touch.

What started out as an appeasement to curiosity quickly turned into something else.

Perhaps Zola was on to something. Why not experiment with this man, the first one to truly attract her? It wouldn't hurt anyone.

On the contrary, it felt great.

She sucked him harder, drawing him deeper and deeper. Odd how giving him pleasure heightened her own. Her sex quivered and she knew her panties were soaked.

His husky interruption only made it worse when he said, "Bring that pussy over here so I can return the favor."

He wanted to lick her too? She glanced at him, startled by his demand, and found him staring at her, hunger clear in his heavily-lidded eyes.

"Sit that sweet cunt on my face." His lips curved into a wicked grin and Steph's body shuddered in response.

Now she couldn't help but wonder what it would feel

like to have his mouth on her sex. Licking her. Touching her.

I want it.

Before she could think twice, or talk herself out of it, she shimmied off her shorts, baring her lower body. Mounting the bed, she wasn't quite sure what to do. He guided her.

"69 me, Ariel. Put that sweet pussy over my face and keep sucking my cock."

She knew what a 69 was, and her cheeks heated. But she obeyed. She was too into the sensual act to stop now.

She poised herself over his mouth, and even though she couldn't see his face, squeezed her eyes shut tight, embarrassed at having such an intimate part of her exposed to a stranger.

"Bring it closer," was his husky whisper. "I want to taste you."

Slowly, she lowered herself, only to almost collapse and smother him at his first lick.

She cried out and arched her back, her entire body trembling.

"Bring it back, Ariel," he growled. "I was just getting started."

She lowered her pussy again, and this time was prepared for the electric shock of his tongue against her.

The decadent pleasure of it.

Her fingers clawed at the sheets as he licked and when her face dipped, his bobbing cock hit her in the chin.

His cock. Right. She wrapped her lips around him and began to suck. She tried to match his pace on her sex.

But got distracted. Moaned a lot. Not that he seemed to mind. He was rock hard and he groaned too.

The orgasm shook her like a hurricane. Hitting her hard and fast.

She screamed around the cock in her mouth. Cried out and trembled and shook as he wrung pleasure out of her. A pleasure that didn't end.

She wanted to whimper when he finally stopped lapping at her and said, "Get on my cock."

By now she was past thinking. Past anything but getting more of this pleasure.

Turning around, she straddled him until the tip of his cock nudged her sex.

It's too big.

"No it's not," he said.

It startled her to realize she'd spoken out loud.

Slowly, she lowered herself onto his dick, so slowly, feeling him as he stretched the entrance to her sex, the pressure breathtaking.

"That's it. Sit that sweet cunt down on my cock. You're so fucking sweet and tight."

His dirty words made her shudder and she slid down a bit further, only to squeak in surprise at a sudden sharp pain as his dick hit her maidenhead.

It never even occurred to her to get off as she dug her nails into his chest and slammed the rest of the way down.

CHAPTER TEN

SHE'S A FUCKING VIRGIN!

Of all the messed up shit that had happened thus far, that ranked even higher than the surprise seduction.

He might have thought she faked it, except he goddam well felt it when he pushed through that barrier, saw her grimace of pain as she bit her lip and soldiered through.

What he couldn't figure out was why she'd done it?

He also didn't care because with her wrapped snugly around his cock, he was in heaven.

The moist walls of her channel gripped him tight, the heat of her and lingering spasms of her orgasm had his body taut.

If he wasn't careful he'd come.

And what's the problem with that?

She wasn't ready to come with him. And for some strange reason, that mattered.

Fully seated on him, she didn't move, her face adopting an expression more of concentration than bliss.

"What are you doing?" he asked through gritted teeth. More like what wasn't she doing? She was the one in control. The one on top. It was up to her to do the work.

And no, he didn't have a problem with her seducing him. Why would he prevent the pleasure she seemed intent on giving? Hell, he'd licked her until she came on his tongue because, despite the situation, she attracted him.

Even the fact she used him now as her first lover—only lover, which was a powerful arousing fact on its own—didn't cool his ardor. Nor did it mean he wouldn't punish her when he got free.

Good sex wouldn't save her.

Her brow creased and her bottom lip got sucked between her teeth. "This feels odd."

"The correct terminology is it feels good."

"No, it's odd. And very full. You might be splitting me in two. It's hard to tell."

It was hard, all right, and her very innocence didn't make things easier. "I promise you'll like it if you ride me."

"I don't know how."

For some reason, this made his cock jerk inside her and she noticed it. Her eyes widened.

"Just move. There is no wrong way. Whatever feels good, just keep doing it." The irony of giving lessons to his captor was almost laugh-worthy. Almost. But balls deep in her, he didn't feel like laughing at all.

She wiggled. "Like this."

He sucked in a breath.

"I'm doing this wrong, aren't I?"

"No," he managed to gasp. "You're doing just fine. Keep it up and you'll see."

"Are you sure?" She squirmed some more, driving him deeper, and her nails, which had relaxed, dug into him again.

"You're doing just fine. Rock your hips on me."

She obeyed, her eyes shutting as she slowly rotated on top him. He undulated his hips upwards, driving himself deeper into her. Saw how her breath caught.

"Untie me, Ariel," he whispered. "Let me properly teach you."

Her eyes flashed open. "Tell me what I want to know."

Was this why she was seducing him? "I'll tell you if you free me."

"You'll tell me or I'll stop." She paused atop him. The moist flesh of her cunt squeezing. And in that moment, weak or not, he would have spilled everything he knew.

If he knew.

But he didn't and he didn't like ultimatums.

"If you want to know, you'll have to torture me some more."

"You would rather I hurt you?"

"I mean," he arched his hips, "I'd rather you torture me some more like this."

"It hurts?"

"More than you can imagine." Because he had to hold himself back. Hold himself from spilling inside her. Even though she sat still, his cock pulsed.

Suspicion crept into her eyes. "I think you're lying."

"I think you don't know what game you're playing, Ariel."

"Tell me what I need to know." Her nails dug into him as she leaned forward. Her cunt squeezed tight and she ground against him, perhaps new to the game, but catching on quick.

"You want information then you're going to have to give me more, Ariel. Show me how much you want this." She ground herself against him and he gasped. "That's it, but if you want to really torture me, you're gonna have to ride. Up and down, Ariel. Let me feel your slick cunt rubbing the length of my cock."

"Like this?" She lifted herself up, drawing her sex away before she bounced down, sucking him back in. Then up again. Down.

Fuck.

Yes.

A low moan slipped past his lips. "Yes. That's it. Faster."

And faster. Her eyes shut again as she rode him, bouncing on his dick, grinding against him, her breath coming fast and harsh.

His own panted along with her. He almost forgot she'd tied him up. Almost forgot she did this to use him.

Who cared, when he'd never felt anything so freaking amazing?

The slick friction made his pleasure coil. His dick throbbed, achingly hard. He held on with gritted teeth. For some reason, he didn't want to be selfish and come alone. No matter her reasons, she'd given him a gift. Her innocence, something she would always remember. He owed it to her, to mankind, to make it good.

So fucking good.

He held on and watched her through heavy-lidded eyes as she bounced. He observed as her breathing drew short and her skin flushed. Reveled in her mewling cries as her climax approached.

"Lean forward," he encouraged, knowing she needed to change the angle to come. Needed that extra pressure on her clit.

With sweat pearling on her body, she leaned forward, her hands sliding to grip his shoulders, her breasts, hidden by her shirt, pressing into his chest.

The new rocking motion pushed her over the edge, and as he thrust into her climbing that same peak, he felt her climax on his cock. The solid fisting of his shaft, a grip so tight he yelled, just as she screamed.

All the muscles in her channel spasmed in undulating waves around his cock as he exploded inside her.

It was the most intense sex he'd ever had.

What a shame he'd probably end up killing her.

CHAPTER ELEVEN

Collapsing on him, it took Steph a moment to recover.

A second longer for the holy shit embarrassment to set in.

Then cold reality and the reason why she'd started the seduction slapped her. Head resting on his chest, hearing his heart racing just as fast as hers, she whispered, "Please. Tell me where my brother is."

"No."

She shoved herself up and glared at him. "I gave you what you wanted. Now tell me."

"You took what you wanted. I just went along for the ride." And looked mighty cocky about it.

A spark of anger made her terse. "You said you'd tell me."

"I lied."

"You asshole!" She slapped him, not just because he'd fooled her, but because the idiocy of what she'd just done hit her.

I just lost my virginity to this jerk and for what? Nothing. He still wouldn't talk.

She peeled herself off him and ignored his teasing. "Does this mean we're not trying for another round? Give me a few minutes and I'll be good to go again."

"If you can't give me what I need then what's the point?"

"I don't know. I'd say I gave you exactly what you needed."

"You gave me an orgasm. Whoop-de-doo."

"I fucked you, Ariel. And you loved it."

She canted her head. "It was okay, I guess. Now I have a basis of comparison for the next time."

For some reason, his nostrils flared. "Already planning your next abduction and seduction?"

"Now that I've gotten that pesky virgin thing out of the way, I doubt I'll need to go to extremes. I can have my pick of men."

"No one will ever compare to me, Ariel," he growled. "I've ruined you for anyone else."

"I highly doubt that. Although, I do admire the balls on you, the cocky ones, not the hairy pair."

"I'm not that hairy."

"Says you. I'm going to leave now."

"Don't you dare. We're not done."

She cast him a glance and smirked. "I am. Later, gator."

"Ariel!" He thrashed. "Untie me, goddammit. Stop fucking with me."

"A second ago you wanted me to fuck you again. And they say women can't make up their minds. While I'm gone, you might want to rethink your decision to stay silent."

"I'm going to kill you!" he bellowed as he strained at the ropes.

Ignoring his threats, Steph left her captive, snaring her shorts on the way. She didn't put them on, not yet. On deck, dawn was breaking, and Zola was nowhere in sight.

Wasn't there to witness her shame. To help guide her through her confusion.

I gave myself to him. A man who hated her, and with reason. She kind of hated herself right now, too.

The shorts she dangled hit the deck. She couldn't put those back on yet. Semen and blood leaked down her thighs, and the sight of it made her blood run cold.

Shit. He came inside me. And she wasn't on any kind of birth control.

Surely one time wouldn't matter? She could almost feel the slap upside the head with Zola muttering, "Idiot."

It only took once. Maybe she'd get lucky and it wouldn't take root.

What of the next time?

There would be no next time. Not with him at any rate—even if she wanted more. *The pleasure, dear God. I never imagined it would be so good.*

It could never happen again.

Life in the compound, with its sometimes meager resources, had taught her to make do without. Steph knew how to ration herself, whether with food or pleasure. There would be no more sex with her captive. From now on, it would be strictly business.

Stripping her shirt, she dove into the ocean, the water sluicing all signs of her depravity from her skin.

However, it couldn't erase what she'd done. What *they'd* done.

I'm not a virgin anymore.

Oddly, she didn't feel any different. Shouldn't she have changed? Would it show when people looked at her?

Head breaking the surface of the waves, she flipped her hair out of her face and blinked back water.

Zola stood leaning against the rail, towel in hand. "So?" she queried.

"He still won't tell me where Ronin is."

"Don't be a dipshit. I meant how did it go?"

Playing deliberately obtuse, Steph replied, "I just told you he wouldn't talk."

"Don't you make me beat you for it."

A grin crested her lips. "Bully. Since you insist on knowing, it went good."

"Only good?"

Steph shrugged as she treaded water. "It was great. You happy? I'm not a giant virgin anymore."

"About time."

"Says the woman who threatened everyone's balls if they so much as looked at me."

"Stop your bitching, and get your ass out of that water. We don't need you attracting the wrong sorts with your popped cherry blood."

Swinging up the short ladder, Steph clambered onto the boat and grabbed the towel. She scrubbed her skin dry. "Whatcha doing up at this hour?" she asked.

"Hard to sleep with all that yelling. Sounded like he did pretty good for a man all tied up."

Her cheeks heated. "You heard?"

"How could I not? The pair of you weren't exactly quiet."

"Sorry."

"Don't be sorry. Seems as if your first time was better than most. Lucky girl."

"It would have been luckier if your plan had worked. He still won't tell me shit about Ronin."

"So, you keep trying."

"Trying how? I already had sex with him." And more.

"Kill him with kindness. Have more sex if you have to."

"Isn't that wrong?" she asked with a wrinkled nose.

"Do you want to find your brother?"

"Yes, but—"

"Then do what you have to. And if you don't, I will."

Not knowing if Zola meant seduction or torture, she flattened her lips. "I can do this." She had to, for Ronin.

The next time she went down below, she brought a damp cloth and a tray of food. She tried to ignore the flutter of her heart. She might be determined to use Gavin for her own ends, but that did nothing to stem her excitement at being near him again.

As soon as she entered the cabin, his eyes opened and he turned his head to watch her.

"And she returns," he said in a low monotone, his clear blue eyes tracking her movements.

"I brought some food. Hungry?" she asked. Her gaze dropped to stare at the floor as a strange shyness invaded her.

"Depends on what you're offering."

"I've got some soup and crackers."

"I'd prefer something sweeter."

Her gaze met his and the glitter in his eyes made her breath hitch. "Did you want me to grab you some fruit?"

"I want another lick at that spot between your thighs."

Not the answer she expected. Red heat crept into her cheeks.

Give it to him.

A part of her was tempted.

She ignored it, instead sitting on the bed, the tray balanced on her lap. It was then she realized feeding him soup was a dumb idea. He was lying flat. So instead she gave him crackers, hand feeding him as he watched her, his lips half curved in a smile, a strangely intimate moment.

Avoiding his gaze meant looking elsewhere and noticing the mess they'd made of him below the waist.

Standing abruptly, she set the tray down on the table and grabbed the cloth she'd brought. She slapped it on his genitals.

"Gentle, Ariel. I'm going to need it later."

She eased up on the pressure.

"If you'd let me go, I could shower instead. You could join me."

She ignored him and kept washing, while at the same time trying to not notice the thickening of his shaft.

"Giving me the silent treatment? That seems rude given you had your cunt on my face a few hours ago."

She clamped her lips tight.

"Did your partner in crime give you hell for fucking the prisoner?"

"It was her idea," she mumbled.

"Her? Kidnapped by two women? The shame never ends." He groaned, closing his eyes.

"That's pretty sexist," she said, slapping the cloth against him.

"And your indignation is priceless given you used sex against me."

"Not very well, apparently, since it still didn't get me any answers."

"Are you still going on about your brother?"

"I have to find him."

"How did you lose him in the first place?"

"I didn't lose him. He was on a mission."

"What kind of mission?"

"I can't say." Mostly because she didn't know. Some gang jobs weren't common knowledge.

"You don't seem to know much, Ariel. Which begs the question, why me? Why harass me for answers? I doubt very much I know your brother. I prefer to work alone."

"Liar. I saw you with those two guys. You seemed pretty chummy."

"Those morons just happen to work for the same guy I do."

"Who do you work for?" she asked.

"You don't really think I'm going to answer that, do you?"

She flung the cloth, her irritation bubbling over. "Why the hell are you being so stubborn? I just want to know what you did to my brother." Then because she couldn't help it, her voice lowered to add a trembling, "Please."

"You are persistent." Gavin sighed. "And just who is your brother?"

She blinked. "What do you mean who is my brother?" She might have blinked again, and resisted an urge to slap herself. She groaned. "For fuck's sake. I suck at this so bad. Did I not ever mention his name?"

"Nope." He shook his head. "And I will add you still haven't even told me your name."

At this point, it seemed kind of stupid to hide it. "Stephanie. Steph for short. My brother's name is Ronin."

A blank expression met her statement and her stomach sank.

"Big dude. Like huge." She spread her hands. "Covered in tattoos."

"You just described half the people I know."

"He disappeared after talking to you."

"Says who?"

"Someone I questioned."

A sardonic grin pulled his lips. "So, on the basis of some wharf rat giving you my name, you went through this elaborate scheme to kidnap me?" Gavin snorted. "Are you on fucking drugs?"

"Never!"

"And yet you took whoever spilled my name at face value."

"I threatened him."

"So? You threatened me too. I hate to break it to you, Ariel, but you're not very good at it."

"But he seemed so sure." She paced alongside the bed. "Claimed he saw you in that oyster place by the north end of the wharf. Said you guys looked pretty intense."

"Wrong guy, Ariel. I wouldn't eat in that shack if you paid me. I've seen the bribes they've given the health inspector."

She whirled to glare at him. "How do I know you're not lying to me?"

"You don't."

"Then I'm back to square one." She resumed her pacing.

"How can you be sure he's even in trouble? Boys sometimes go off grid to blow some steam."

"Ronin wouldn't. He never goes more than a few days without contacting me."

"How long has it been?

"Nine days."

"Nine days isn't very long in the islands. A proper bender can last weeks."

"He wouldn't do that. Wouldn't just disappear without contacting me. He's always taken care of me since we were little." Ronin took his big brother duties very seriously.

"What about your parents?"

The vague recollections didn't even have faces anymore. She shook her head. "Gone. Killed in the islands when while we were on vacation as kids."

"So you're American?"

She shrugged. "Probably, but no one ever came looking for us. We lived on the streets for a while until Zola found us."

"Who's Zola?"

It occurred to Steph she was doing most of the talking. She frowned at him. "She's none of your business. And I'm beginning to realize we made a hasty mistake. You really don't know Ronin, do you?"

"If you're asking if I've killed any big tattooed dudes lately, other than Meathead from the other night, then the answer is no. I was on a hiatus from work."

"Then this was all for nothing." She'd grabbed the wrong guy.

"Glad we got this cleared up. Now, why don't you be a good girl and set me free?"

She chewed her lower lip. "I want to, but I can't. I don't know if I can trust you. You said before you wanted to kill me."

"Words spoken in the heat of the moment. Surely you can understand. I mean, how would you react if the roles were reversed?"

Not too well, probably. "If it was me, I'd hate you."

"Does that look like I harbor hate?" He indicated his swelling cock.

She stared at it, amazed anew that it even fit inside her. Surely it didn't feel as good as she recalled.

"I want you, Ariel. Let me pleasure you."

"I don't need you for that." Masturbation was everyone's best friend.

"Please, we both know you loved it. The feel of my cock inside you. Filling up your sweet cunt."

She did remember. Wanted.

"The hot lap of my tongue against your clit. I want you to sit on my face again. Coming against my mouth. Then creaming my cock."

"We shouldn't."

"Why deny ourselves the pleasure?"

Why, indeed. She shimmied out of her shorts.

"That's it, Ariel, let me seduce your sweet cunt. Set me free. I want to finger fuck you as I'm licking that clit."

A tremor went through her. It sounded so tempting. But she wasn't completely stupid.

"I don't think untying you is a good idea."

"Then you can forget me getting you off. I won't be used."

"You're in no position to make any demands. And I can do whatever I like." To punctuate her claim, she grasped his cock and squeezed.

"Let me fucking go," he snarled, yanking at his tethers.

She met his gaze and gave him the same reply he'd given her when she asked. "No." She gripped him tighter and he growled, even as his dick pulsed in her fist.

She climbed onto the bed, holding his gaze and his cock.

His eyes blazed and his lips flattened in anger, but he couldn't hide his arousal.

His cock strained, the tip of it pearling with anticipation.

Straddling him, she heard him growl. "Don't you fucking dare. Release me."

"Tell me you don't want this." If he rejected her, she'd walk away.

"Goddamn you, you can see I want it. But not like this."

"Yet this is the only way. So let me ask you again, do you really want me to leave?"

The word "No" was groaned and he bucked, just as she rammed herself down on him.

They both gasped. Her sex was slightly sore from before, but the moisture within lubed his way and she quickly hummed with pleasure as he stretched her.

"I will make you regret this," he snarled even as his hips pumped up into her.

"I already do," she admitted. The strange desire she had for him was inexplicable. Still, she couldn't seem to fight it.

Didn't want to.

She rocked on him, crying out her pleasure while he grunted his. For a man who protested, he was awfully vigorous. Hips thrusting upwards, driving his cock deep. She ground against him, her breath quickening, her body moving quickly to climax.

Beep. Beep. Beep.

An alarm went off and she grimaced as she lost her rocking rhythm. She stilled and he groaned. "Don't stop now, Ariel. I'm right fucking there."

So was she, but an alarm usually didn't bode well.

A shout came from above. "Ariel, get your ass on deck. We have company."

Fuck.

She hopped off Gavin and wiggled back into her shorts as she shouted back, "I'm coming. Who is it? Coast guard? Fucking tourists?" They were everywhere in the islands.

"I don't know, but they're not responding to my hails and they're headed straight at us." Zola stuck her head in the hatch. "We should get moving. You coming?"

The right answer sat on her tongue, and yet it wasn't what she said. "You go on without me. I think I'll stick with him for now. I'm not done questioning him yet." Such a lie. He knew nothing about Ronin, and yet she found herself reluctant to leave.

A knowing smirk crossed Zola's face. "Then you should stick around a while longer. Torture him for more info." Even bigger smirk. "I'm gonna try leading them away."

"Them? Is there more than one?" Steph asked.

"Two coming in on opposite sides. We gotta move before they box us in."

"It might just be pleasure cruisers." Then again, in these waters, it could also be pirates.

"Maybe. Maybe not. Let's see if they take the bait and follow. Are you sure you can handle this one on your own?"

Steph knew Zola meant the boat, but for some reason, she replied, "I can take care of him."

"Stay safe and remember, if it's pirates, don't let them take you alive." Because there were fates worse than death.

Zola ducked out, and Steph went to follow. She needed to reel in the anchor and get the motor going.

"Let me go. I can help."

She peered back at him, naked and splayed on the bed, his expression concerned.

"I can handle your ship."

"But can you handle pirates on your own?"

"We don't know it's pirates. And even if it is, I can fight."

"I know you can, but I'd rather not die because you're trying to prove some feminist point."

"Whereas I'd rather not give in to your goading and end up dead because you're lying to me."

"Would I kill the woman I was just fucking?"

"You tell me."

He smiled. "We aren't done."

The promise in his words held such heat. "I gotta go." But she didn't move, caught in a staring match.

Crack. The gunshot echoed loudly across the water and he swore. "Stop being so fucking stubborn. Two of us stand a better chance than one. And I know this ship better than anyone."

A very good point. "Promise you won't hurt me."

"How about I do one better and promise I won't kill you. I want to live as much as you do, Ariel. If it makes you feel better, you can tie me up after we escape and have your wicked way again." He arched a brow.

"This is such a bad idea," she muttered, and yet she still pulled out her knife and sliced through the rope and the zip tie.

Without waiting to see what he'd do, she sprinted out of the cabin to the deck and launched herself at the anchor, reeling it in as fast as she could. The motor roared to life just as another pop of gunfire exploded. It pinged off the railing and she instinctively ducked.

The anchor hit the deck with a wet thump. A strand of seaweed caught on it slapped her bare foot.

"Anchor's up," she yelled.

Gavin didn't reply, but she could see him in the wheelhouse, expression grim as he revved the motor. The yacht lurched into motion, and she staggered. This wasn't her first stint on a rocky boat, though, and she caught her balance.

Gripping the rail, she peered off into the distance, the sunshine bouncing off the waves, making it hard for her to discern the shape of the boat bearing down on them.

"Incoming to our aft," she shouted on her way to the wheelhouse. She joined Gavin who stood there in a pair of trousers he'd donned and nothing else.

Since he stood at the helm, his hands capably

steering the boat, she got to admire the rippling muscles. A different perspective from his previous position flat on his back. It brought home just how much bigger and wider than her he was.

If he lied to me, I might not stand much of a chance. She already knew he could fight. Then again, so could she. However, he would have the edge with his size and strength.

She'd have to trust in his word. A promise from a known scumbag. Not exactly comforting, but all she had.

The yacht picked up speed, slicing through the ocean waters, the swells causing it to jump as Gavin sought to put distance between them and their pursuers.

"Can we outrun them?" she asked glancing behind.

Pop. Pop. Pop. They both ducked as the approaching ship peppered them with bullets.

"We might have gotten away if someone had released me sooner," he grumbled. He stood and his muscles bulged as he tried to keep the boat on course at high speed.

"Well excuse me," she snapped. "Maybe this wouldn't have happened if you'd parked somewhere a little safer."

He barked out a laugh. "There is nowhere truly safe in the Caribbean, Ariel."

"What do you think they want?" she asked.

"Given my boat's not exactly a shining prize, and my hold is empty, I'm going to guess someone is looking for a bounty."

"On you?"

"Don't sound so surprised. I'm a wanted man in many places."

"Ah yes, Crusty Seadog, the scourge of the mainland, and drug runner extraordinaire."

"Who the fuck told you that?" he exclaimed.

"I told you I knew your name from that fight by the bar. Everyone in the crowd heard it."

"And this informant of yours, he told you to look for me?"

"Not exactly time for a conversation," she noted as the ship soared over a wave and hit with a shudder. "But yes. The scumbag lied to me and said Ronin was last seen with Crusty Seadog."

"I'll be damned," he muttered mostly to himself. "We'll discuss that later. You might want to grab us some guns."

"I have one."

She grabbed at her shorts only to groan as he said in a mocking tone, "You mean the one in my pants? You forgot it in the cabin and I thought it might come in handy."

She could have slapped herself for being so careless. "Give it back."

"Take it."

Expecting him to react, she was tense as she grabbed the pistol from his waistband. To her surprise, he didn't flinch or look back.

"I assume you know how to shoot that thing?" he asked, the muscles on his arms cording as he spun the boat sharply.

With nothing to hold onto but him, her free hand clutched at his body, the bare skin of his upper body warm beneath her fingers.

"I can shoot." She didn't mention the part that she'd only ever shot wooden targets, not real people.

"Whatever you do," he said, the boat completing its turn to face back in the direction they were fleeing, "don't hesitate."

"We're going to fight?" She might have squeaked the words. Not out of fear. Adrenaline coursed through her veins. This was what she'd trained for.

"We can't outrun them because you waited too long." The reproach in his voice stung.

A childish urge to stick out her tongue came over her. She didn't curb it. Screw him, she didn't owe him any apologies.

Despite facing forward, he remarked, "Be prepared to use that tongue later once we win this fight."

Before she could reply, more gunshots cracked, and she ducked low to the floor. She couldn't help but worry about Gavin who stood tall at the helm, directing the ship.

He slammed something on the dash, and the engine abruptly cut out, leaving only the whine of the other boat as it charged towards them.

"Brace yourself," he warned, ducking beside her.

The impact had a stomach churning sound to it, a screeching of metal on metal that no one ever wanted to hear at sea. She winced, wondering at the damage—*oh my God are we gonna sink?*—as the attacking vessel broadsided them.

Its engine cut out. Over the creaks and groans from the tangled ships, she heard shouts. "They're in the wheelhouse. Kill them both."

"They should have brought a bigger army," Gavin muttered as he leaned forward and pulled out a machete from under the dash.

"What's the plan?" she asked.

"Impress you with my fighting abilities."

"I can fight, too."

"Fight, yes, but can you kill? If your girly sensibilities won't allow it, then stay hidden while I take care of the man's work."

Her jaw dropped. "Man's work? We'll see who kills the most pirates."

A wicked smile tilted his lips. "You're on."

With those words, he dove out of the wheelhouse, yelling as he went.

His unexpected appearance caused chaos.

She heard a gun go off. Screaming. Thumping. The boat rocked.

And she was being a chickenshit.

She stood up and took stock of the fight on deck. Gavin was engaged with two thugs. One she recognized from their last port as Meathead's progeny.

The widow wasn't letting the murder of her husband go.

Crack.

The gunfire came from the other ship, splintering part of the yacht's deck. Turning, she noted the gunman, feet spread, weapon aimed, the rocking of the boats messing with his aim.

Know what else would mess with his shot? *Pop.* She fired off a few rounds, her aim also skewed by the motion of the boats, but she'd accomplished what she needed to.

He no longer stood taking potshots, but hid behind the equipment on deck.

Time to take the fight to the pirates.

Uttering her own battle cry, Steph dove out of the wheelhouse and hit the deck. Slid in a puddle of blood.

Good thing. The machete sliced past her head and into the pirate behind her.

He gurgled and clutched at the blade, yanking it with him as he fell.

She gaped for a moment at his wide open eyes. His very dead eyes.

"Don't just sit there," Gavin yelled.

It snapped her out of it in time to raise her arm to block an incoming blow from a second pirate. Before the thug could try and hit her again, she fired right through his thigh, the close confines of their fight meaning the bullet tore a hole through his leg.

Hard to feel bad about it considering he was about to swing at her with his knife.

Standing, she easily avoided the flailing edge of the blade, and hardening her heart, shot again.

The body went still.

After that, it was easier. A cold clarity settled upon her as she fought alongside Gavin.

Some of those they faced—about six by her count—had guns, but those proved unwieldy with rocking boats and close confines. She ended up snaring a knife, pried from fingers not yet gone rigid in death.

She slashed, parried, and thrust, feeling the hot spray of blood on her face.

The wild adrenaline surged as she fought for her life.

The savage victory when everyone was dead.

And only two were left standing.

Her chest heaving, she found herself facing Gavin in utter silence but for the creaking of the ships. The slick sheen of blood coating them both should have been a deterrent, and yet, it wasn't their blood.

It was the sign of their victory.

We're alive.

His eyes glittered as he took a step toward her, and she must have moved, as well, because a moment later, she found herself pressed against him.

They shared their first kiss. A hot scorcher of an embrace.

The knife fell out of her loose fingers, hitting the deck point first. Not that she cared as she clutched him close.

A moan escaped her when he ran his tongue against the seam of her lips.

She complied when he ordered her to, "Open for me."

The sinuous slide of his tongue wrought a shiver, a pleasurable shaking of every inch of her body.

His hands clasped her by the ass, kneading her flesh as he pulled her hard against him, the distinct line of his erection pressing against her lower belly. The erotic nature of the kiss made her mindless.

She said not a word, didn't want to, when her back hit the outside wall of the cabin.

The sound of tearing fabric only heightened her arousal.

He thrust into her savagely, firmly. It was rough, without much foreplay, and yet it was exactly what she wanted. What she needed.

She hissed, "Yes!" as she clawed at his shoulders. She wanted him to take her. To fuck her. And he did, his thrusts quick and deep.

His fingers dug into her cheeks. Her pleasure mounted and spiraled out of control.

When she screamed, it was in his mouth, her entire

body convulsing and clenching. Her sex fisting his cock as he spurted hotly inside her.

Then leaned his forehead against hers.

A strangely intimate moment of hot pants, sweaty bodies, and subsiding tremors.

When he finally set her down, her legs wobbled, but he didn't see it, having turned away from her.

She held herself steady, one hand braced on the wall.

What just happened?

She looked at the deck, the bodies, the blood. A stark contrast to the ebbing climax.

"We should clear these off before they attract too much attention." His words snapped her out of her daze. Slapped her with their coldness.

What did she expect? A cuddle. Soft words?

Her movements robotic, she helped him drag the corpses to the side where he heaved them over. She watched as he put a hole in the other ship, sending it to a watery grave.

She manned the pump as he flushed the deck of remaining blood. Screeched when he turned the hose first on her, then himself, rinsing them clean.

"Toss your clothes." One of the few things he'd said since they started the cleanup. Then again, what was there to say?

That death was messy?

That she must be depraved to have indulged in toe-curling sex right after?

She suspected she suffered from shock.

Snap out of it.

She needed to do something to reassert herself with

this man who'd so quickly taken charge. Yet, something kept her quiet.

Stripping, she tossed her garments into the sea, too numb to feel embarrassed that she stood there naked on his deck.

He gripped her, his hands closing vise tight around her forearms. He lifted her and began walking.

It finally snapped her out of her shock long enough to say, "What are you doing?"

"Ever heard the expression an eye for an eye?"

"You said you wouldn't kill me," she exclaimed.

"I don't plan to." He grinned, and yet the expression held no mirth.

"This wasn't the deal," she said, finally coming to life. She struggled in his grip, but as she feared, his strength was no match for her size.

Use your head. More like use her feet. She tucked them up and swung, hitting him in the balls.

He bellowed and dropped her.

As she hit the deck, she wasted no time, sprinting to the side of the boat and diving into the warm ocean water.

And probably to her death.

CHAPTER TWELVE

Did she seriously just jump off the ship?

He was tempted to leave her in the ocean. Let her drown. He didn't care.

He was free and she would pay for her temerity.

Except death by drowning meant he wouldn't get the pleasure of torturing her like she tortured him.

He dove in after her.

She swam well, he'd give her that, but he was raised in the water. Had even swum competitively for a time during his teens.

He caught her by the ankle and yanked, submerging her. She broke the surface of the water, sputtering.

"Let me go, asshole," she screeched, kicking her legs.

He released her ankle only so he could get a better grip on her body. His hands easily spanned her waist as he yanked her nude body close.

"I told you we weren't done."

"I'll kill you. I can do it. You saw me. I'm not afraid," she ranted.

He couldn't help but recall her during the fight.

How she'd looked. Savage. Efficient. Skilled. Then after. Glowing with adrenaline. He'd not been able to help himself.

He'd fucked her while their blood still ran hot from the battle.

But then came the shock. The glazed look in her eyes, the robotic movements as she'd helped him clean up.

It touched something inside him. Something long buried. Weak.

He had to fight that weakness. Fight her allure.

He wasn't sure what he'd planned when he grabbed her. Although, the idea of tying her up did tantalize.

Now, in the water, she didn't make it easy, her lithe body slippery. But she was no match for brute strength.

He managed to wrap an arm around her neck, and while she clawed at his forearm, he swam them back to the boat. It took some maneuvering to heave them both on board. She kicked and scratched every inch of the way.

Once on deck, she face him, half crouched, her hair hanging partially in her face, her fingers crooked, her lips peeled in a snarl.

Naked.

He'd never seen anything more desirable in his life. And she noticed his interest.

"Don't you dare bring that thing anywhere near me," she snapped as he stalked towards her.

"That's not what you were screaming the last time. As I recall, you couldn't stop saying 'yes, yes, yes,' as I fucked you."

"Momentary lack of reason."

"I agree. So don't think the fact I liked fucking you will ease your punishment."

"What happened to not hating me?" she asked, keeping pace with him on the deck, moving as he moved, staying out of reach.

"I don't hate you, Ariel. But,"—he lunged and got a fistful of hair, reeling her in until he could anchor an arm around her waist—"I will have my revenge. Don't worry, I did promise I wouldn't kill you. However, I never said it wouldn't hurt."

"Bastard," she hissed as he lifted her. "I'm going to carve your balls from your body and feed them to the fish."

"This talk about my balls really gives me an urge to teabag." When she quieted, he laughed. "You have no idea what that means."

"Whatever it is, you can forget it."

He chuckled softly against her ear as he heaved her off the deck. "I'm going to teach you so many things, Ariel."

"Not today, you're not," said a new voice.

The blow from behind dropped him.

When he regained consciousness, with a lump on the back of his head, he cursed. He knew the truth even before he searched his ship.

Ariel was gone.

For some reason, he found that utterly unacceptable. He tried to convince himself that it was for the best.

He didn't make a policy of killing women, even ones that aggravated him. And yet, he couldn't forget her.

Couldn't stop picturing those vivid green eyes.

Couldn't help recalling the tight clamp of her sex.

He'd taken her virginity. Introduced her to the pleasures of sex.

Now she was gone, free to fuck anyone she chose. To touch another man. To come and scream the name of another.

It ignited a jealous spark and a strange possessiveness.

She belongs to me.

He had to get her back.

CHAPTER THIRTEEN

It had been two days since her rescue. Zola had used the beacon on the ship to find her. She still wasn't sure how Zola managed to sneak up on them.

Then again, she and Gavin had been so busy sparring, they might not have noticed a cannon going off.

I wonder what he would have done to me.

He blew hot and cold, and fucked like a god. Then again, having only ever slept with him, she could only assume he did it well. She'd have to sleep with another guy to truly compare.

Now if only other guys attracted her.

It wasn't for a lack of looking. Zola had sailed them to a new island, St. Lucia. A new place to look for Ronin.

This time, Zola came along with her to question their targets. But none of them had anything to say.

None of them evoked anything other than irritation that they couldn't give her what she wanted.

Only Gavin could give her what she needed.

Sigh.

She'd been doing that a lot since their separation.

You'd almost think I missed him. Which was stupid. How could she miss a jerk who'd probably forgotten her the moment she left?

Her attitude didn't go unnoticed.

Zola pursed her lips and more than once threatened. *"Stop your moping. He's just a man. There are plenty of others."*

She knew that, yet that didn't stop her from dreaming of him. It angered her that he consumed her thoughts, especially since her only focus should be finding her brother. But the more she looked, the more hopeless it seemed. No one knew anything. Not one person saw anything.

And so she even resorted to asking about Crusty Seadog. After all, she knew his word was worthless. Perhaps he'd lied about Ronin. He'd lied about everything else.

What she learned about him didn't reassure.

He was a cold-blooded killer.

A womanizer.

A drug runner.

And so much more.

The stories she heard painted a man with no mercy, no conscience, and oddly enough, he didn't sound like Gavin at all because people seemed to universally agree that he was a dirty fighter. A guy who preferred a knife in the back or a bullet from afar. Not one who fought with his fists.

Strange. Then again, what could you expect with rumors?

"Snap out of it, dawta. This is the place."

Steph slowed her steps and noted they'd halted before A Tavern of Ill Repute.

Seriously, that was the name carved in the sign hanging above the door.

As they entered, several pairs of eyes rotated towards them, peering through the haze of cigarette and other smoke. Male eyes that showed interest in women who weren't garbed as whores.

They took a seat at a table sticky with rings of spilled drinks. Steph leaned back in her seat and took stock of the people in the room.

"Who do you think I should hit?" she asked her foster mother.

"Your guess is as good as mine at this point," Zola replied, raising her fingers and indicating two beers.

A needle in an ocean. This quest to find her brother was turning out to be hopeless. But she couldn't let despair make her give up. Ronin wouldn't.

"What about the scruffy one in the corner?"

Zola didn't turn her head, instead relying on the mirror behind the bar to peek. She shook her braids. "I shook him up already. The only thing he knows is his sister is banging the mayor of this town and his wife."

So many secrets, none of them the right ones. "Any suggestions then?"

"You could try the big one by the bar. He's got that look about him."

"The kind that says he'd sell out his mother?" Steph replied, giving him a once-over.

"He's got the bulk to handle someone like Ronin. And he's wearing a gang tattoo," Zola remarked. "He's also not half bad looking."

"Meaning what?"

"Meaning it's time you forgot that Crusty fellow and tried someone new."

"Just because I popped my cherry doesn't mean I'm in the mood to start humping every man I meet."

"What if I told you the shirt he's wearing is your brother's?"

"What?" Steph stared hard at the man. Frowned. "It's a plain white t-shirt."

"Ronin has one just like it."

Steph glared at Zola. "This isn't funny."

"Wasn't laughing. You need to snap out of it."

"I'm fine."

"You're not fine. You're pining over that guy."

"Don't blame me for that. You're the one who told me to seduce him for answers."

"I didn't say to fall for the guy."

"I did not fall for him."

"Prove it."

Too late Steph saw the trap Zola laid. When a person was dared, there was only one thing to do. Guzzle her beer, slam down the bottle, stand, and declare, "Fine. I'll show you he doesn't mean a thing."

Strutting to the bar, she squared her shoulders. A part of her wanted to say "fuck this" and leave. She didn't want to flirt with this stranger.

Then again, she also wanted to stop thinking about Gavin.

Stopping at the bar, she leaned against it. It took only a second for the big guy sitting there to notice her.

"Well, hello there," he drawled, his gravelly voice not making her tingle at all like Gavin's had. "I don't think I've seen you around here before." He didn't even try to hide his interest as his eyes roved her frame.

Again, no tingles. Rather an urge to slap him for ogling her. That and a need for a shower.

Why was it the overt stares and innuendos left her feeling dirty? "I'm looking for someone."

"I'd say your search is over." The leer was probably supposed to be sexy. The guy wasn't ugly; he had a chiseled face, a five o'clock shadow, and a pleasant smell that indicated he believed in bathing.

"Flattered, but not interested." Steph didn't couch her words. "I'm looking for my brother."

"And you think I've seen him?" The guy leaned back on his stool, trusting in the spindly backrest.

"You tell me. His name is Ronin. Big fellow. Covered in tats."

"Sounds familiar."

"It does?" She couldn't help but sound surprised.

"It does. I'd hate to get your hopes up, though."

"Where did you see him?"

"I think it was the mainland. Some bar…" He stared off for a moment before snapping his fingers. "Shit, I can't remember the name of it. Some new place on the beach. I've got matches for it up in my room if you want them."

It took restraint to prevent her eyes from rolling at his obvious attempt to get her in bed. "I don't appreciate your bullshitting me." She shoved away from him, only to find her arm gripped by his meaty hand.

"No bullshit, sweetheart. I saw your brother. He doesn't have red hair like you, though. But I'll bet you're the Stephanie he's got etched into that tattoo of a heart."

Her breath hitched. "You saw him."

"I told you I did, and if you come with me, I'll get you those matches. Or stay here since you think I'm so desperate for pussy that I need to lie to a chick to get her to my room."

She shrugged. "Can you blame me?"

He chuckled. "Not really. I know a lot of guys who'd do or say anything to get in your pants. Wait here. I'll grab it."

"I'll come with you." Because Zola was right. Perhaps she should be checking out other guys. This one, while not making her heart pitter-patter, wasn't an obvious asshole.

He at least didn't have a problem spilling the goods without threats or seduction. That surely deserved something in return.

Am I really going to have sex with him?

It might show her that Gavin wasn't the only one who could make her body sing.

Or further cement the fact that he had ruined her for other men.

"You're staying over the tavern?" she asked as she followed him through a door and up a set of stairs.

"Renting it for a few days while I conduct business. Name's Viper, by the way." He tossed her a glance over his shoulder. Had to admire the balls on him, letting a stranger walk behind him.

"I'm Steph."

"Anyone tell you it's probably not a good idea to solicit strangers for info about your brother?"

"I don't really have any other options." She didn't mention the fact she wasn't alone.

"It's nice you care about your brother." Viper slapped a keycard against an electronic lock. A surprise in this place. The door opened and he said, "You can stay out in the hall if you'd like while I grab it."

The mere fact he offered had her stepping over the threshold, only to realize as she looked around this place was more than a stopping point rented by the day or hour.

She whirled, but the door had already slammed shut and Viper leaned against it.

"Move away from the door." She had a knife at her hip, but she still hoped she'd misconstrued his actions.

He shook his head. "Not until you show me the goods."

"I thought you didn't need to coerce women for sex."

"I don't. You're going to be very cooperative. Or else. Take off your shirt."

"No." She took a step back, but wasn't fast enough. His hand lashed out and he grabbed her by the throat.

He exerted just enough pressure to cut off her air, and lifted her on tiptoe.

"I said, take off the shirt."

He released her and she gasped for air. She thought about going for her knife, but thought it better if she waited for the element of surprise.

I need to distract him.

So she gave him what he asked for. She tugged off her shirt, leaving her clad only in a sports bra. Not exactly lacy lingerie, but it did outline her breasts and give her some cleavage.

A hungry glitter entered Viper's eyes. As he perused her, he muttered, "Very nice."

"I gave you what you asked for. Give me the matches." Despite his vile tactics, he'd obviously seen her brother.

He pulled them from his pocket.

Lying bastard had them the entire time.

He dangled them over his head. "You're going to have to give me more if you want these. Come here and give me a kiss."

She clamped her lips shut. She wouldn't whore herself.

Why not, you did it with Gavin?

But Gavin didn't make her feel dirty. Gavin didn't force her to do shit.

I forced him.

The realization hit her hard as she understood how he must have felt.

But he enjoyed it.

That didn't make it right.

"Tick tock, sweetheart. I'm not going to wait all night. You want these, you're going to have to give me something in return."

I'll give you something, all right. Her knife in his gut. But she'd have to get closer.

She closed the distance, and tried not to flinch or attack when he reached out to grab her about the waist and draw her in.

"You're just a tiny thing," he murmured. "I'm gonna enjoy spinning you on my dick."

He leaned down, intent on kissing her. Steph recoiled, her stomach tight with repugnance. She turned her head and his lips pressed a kiss to her cheek instead.

The warm breath of his chuckle brushed her skin. "Come on, sweetheart. One little kiss."

"Then what? I'm not a whore."

"Which is what makes this so exciting. But how about I give you something. A gesture of good faith."

One hand released her only to tuck something in her cleavage.

I've got the matchbook!

"Your turn."

She smiled up at him. "Yes, it is my turn." Like other guys before him, he only saw a weak woman, someone soft and vulnerable.

He didn't see the knife.

But she'd miscalculated his reflexes. She yanked her blade free of its sheath and aimed for his gut, only to have her wrist caught and bent back.

She cried out and the blade hit the floor with a clatter.

"That wasn't very nice. Guess you'll have to make it up to me." With a rough shove, he slammed her against the wall, his heavier body pressing against hers.

If he'd expected her to cow to his show of force, he thought wrong.

Anger tightened her frame. She shifted into survival mode, sifting through possible actions instead of blindly reacting.

He ground himself against her. "I am getting the impression you like it rough." He reached up and squeezed her breast, hard enough to hurt—but unlike Gavin, it didn't excite. "So do I."

"You're disgusting," she spat. *And I'm an idiot.* She'd grown up among men and boys who respected her, never hurt her. The real world was a vastly different place and despite Zola's warnings, it was a shocker to experience it first-hand.

Where was Zola? She could have used her help right about now.

I need to hold him off long enough for her to realize something is wrong.

However, that might prove tricky given he was so strong. Try as she might, she could not dislodge him. Even thrusts of her knees found themselves blocked.

He continued to grope her breast and the more she bucked against him, the more ragged his breath.

"Stop it," she yelled as the situation quickly unraveled.

"Make me," he taunted.

"If you insist, asshole." She lunged forward and bit his chin, the only part of him she could reach. When he yelled and recoiled, she struck out at him, her knee rising to nail him in the balls, his distraction finally allowing her to land a blow.

He bellowed in pain, but released her to cup his balls. She wasted no time and dove for the door. Her fingers were on the knob when he grabbed her by the hair.

"Ow!" She couldn't help but scream as every strand in his fist protested the rough treatment. Rather than let go of the door and slingshot into him, she turned the knob and yanked.

"Oh no, sweetheart. No leaving yet. We've just begun."

He pulled her hand off the door, and holding her hair in one fist, went to shove it shut.

Only it didn't close.

A foot inserted itself in the gap and a familiar voice, cold with fury, said, "Get your fucking hands off her."

Steph could have cried in relief—and her heart stuttered in happiness.

The hand fisted in her hair loosened enough she

could pull free. She staggered away from Viper and hit the floor on her knees.

Whipping her hair out of her face, she turned to see Viper standing at bristling attention.

"This doesn't concern you. Get out."

Gavin—looking more handsome than she recalled—leaned nonchalantly against the door jamb. "I'm making it my concern. Is it me, or does the lady seem unwilling?"

"She's no lady. She approached me in the bar."

"Asking about her brother again, no doubt." Gavin pushed away from the doorframe. "And you thought that was a good enough excuse to manhandle her. Not very nice."

"Still none of your fucking business. Do you know who I am?" Viper growled, his fists clenched at his sides.

"I do, actually. Not that it will matter for much longer. Your kind is a dime a dozen. Quickly forgotten."

"Fuck with me and you're fucking with my boss. He won't take kindly to that."

"And my boss doesn't like bastards who rape women. He also doesn't like a-holes who let their employees abuse them. So, I'll be doing not only my boss a favor, but all of womankind."

"Assuming you can beat me."

"I'd say that was a foregone conclusion." Gavin didn't pull out any weapons, but the way he straightened, his expression dark and dangerous, oozed of confidence. Strength.

It was so fucking sexy, Steph couldn't help the flicker of heat between her thighs.

Where her body was concerned, only one guy could stoke that fire. Gavin.

A man who'd just boldly come to her rescue.

A man who'd only days ago wanted to keep her prisoner for revenge.

Grabbing her knife from the floor, she stood. The asshole in front of her never even bothered to check his back.

Common courtesy didn't extend to his kind.

The knife slid in, easier than expected. Rather than yank it out and make a mess, she stepped away.

"The bitch stabbed me!" Viper whirled and glared at her.

He took a step in her direction, another. She retreated. Those big hands reached for her, but fell away as Gavin pulled out the blade and plunged it in to a fresh spot.

The big guy whirled, roaring, "Motherfucker!"

"What did you expect would happen? I told you to let her go. The woman is mine."

Steph's heart beat faster at Gavin's claim, and yet she couldn't let her emotions cloud her judgment. "I belong to no one."

A snarl curled Gavin's lip as he shot her a heated look. "Think again, Ariel. We have unfinished business. My bunk and the rope are waiting."

For some reason, his words created a pang in her heart. Silly her, she'd thought he'd come looking for her because he missed her. Wanted her. Wrong. He was out for revenge.

Before Steph could say anything in reply, Viper charged Gavin.

Fatal mistake.

Quicker than a viper could stab with its fangs, Gavin moved, grabbing Viper by the head and yanking.

Crack. Viper hit the floor with a heavy thud.

And then it was just Steph and Gavin.

An angry Gavin.

A battle hot man who gazed at her with irritation—and hunger.

Heat suffused her, and wet the crotch of her panties. Desire made her want to dive into his arms.

But that would be foolish.

Save yourself.

She licked her lips and uttered a tremulous, "Thank you."

His eyes darkened, storm clouds brewing in their depths. He closed the space between them while she stood there, trembling.

Trembling with what would happen. What she had to do.

He got close enough to reach and that was when she brought the lamp swinging in an arc and clonked him in head.

She didn't stop to see if he went down.

She ran.

She just didn't make it far.

The door to the hall had remained open and she almost made it to the corridor before slamming into a body. Hands steadied her, and try as she might to thrash and kick, she couldn't break free.

"Let me go," she screeched for the second time that day. However, the implacable grip didn't ease even though she caused her captors to grunt in pain.

"Dammit, Gavin. When you said you needed our help capturing a danger to society, you didn't warn us she'd try and emasculate me," gasped a handsome fellow with dark hair.

"She's feisty," said with a chuckle from the second guy. Kind of a compliment, but his next words made her fume. "I bet she's wild in bed."

"If either of you lay a hand or dick on her, I'll kill you," growled Gavin. "She and I have unfinished business."

"Geezus, no need to get violent. I was just saying."

"Someone's got his balls in a knot," muttered his companion.

"Hand her over," Gavin ordered.

Manhandled from one guy to another didn't sit well with Steph, especially since Gavin seemed so angry. Steph craned to see him over her shoulder. "What are you going to do with me?"

"Do? How about I do to you what you did to me?" he said in a mocking tone.

Have awesome sex? That didn't sound so bad.

Wait, yes it did. "I let you go."

"Only because you had to. If those thugs hadn't come along, how long did you plan to keep me? Hmmm?"

"I did it for my brother."

"Altruistic reasoning doesn't make it right. Which is why I'm going to go on the record saying I'm going to keep you for fun."

"I won't be your whore," she spat.

"Then you shouldn't have acted like one." His voice tight with anger, he leaned in close enough for her to inhale his cologne. "I'm going to seduce you the way you seduced me. Force you to want it. To crave it. I'm going to make you fight your desires, then crumble before them. Over and over."

Click. The cold feel of metal on her wrists had her

eyes opening wide. Another click and her hands were secured together by his friends.

"You bastard!" He'd intentionally distracted her.

"I've been called worse. See you in a bit, Ariel. Think of me like I thought of you when I was tied up." He thrust her from him, and she staggered, only to be caught by one of the other men. "Take her to the yacht and lock her in the cabin," he ordered. "I'll be along in a little bit."

"Whatever you say."

"I think the correct response is aye aye, Captain," replied the other fellow.

"Don't fuck this up. I mean it," Gavin warned.

"His trust in us is lacking, Gunner," said the guy who tossed her over his brawny shoulder."

"Don't cry, Lash. It's not his fault he's daunted by your virile size."

"Out!" bellowed Gavin.

"Definitely small dick syndrome," snickered Lash, the guy holding her upside down. He had an arm braced over her legs preventing her escape.

Her view was restricted to a taut ass covered in patterned swim shorts. She lifted her head to see the one called Gunner following behind.

What she didn't see was Zola anywhere nearby, ready to clobber her captors. Where was her foster mother?

Noticing her glance, Gunner's lips quirked into a smile, and she noticed how attractive and muscular he was. Yet again, while he was good-looking, he elicited nothing more than mild interest from her. Unlike Gavin, who simply had to speak for her panties to get soaked.

Given these fellows seemed to have a more

amenable mien, she tried pleading with them. "Let me go. You don't want to do this."

Laughter made Gunner's teeth gleam. "You know I can't do that. Gavin would totally whoop my ass if we didn't do as he asked."

"I think you could take him." Not really. She'd seen him in action, but Gunner didn't need to know that.

"I am not pitting myself against him. The man is a killing machine. If he wasn't so good at smuggling, he'd have made an epic career as an assassin."

"Dude has some seriously elegant moves," rumbled Lash, joining the conversation.

"Only takes one bullet," she muttered.

"That's not very sporting," Gunner chided. "No wonder he wanted you in cuffs. And, by the way, good job on frazzling him. I don't think I've ever seen him act like this."

"It's because he's pissed I captured him and held him hostage," she retorted.

Gunner's jaw dropped, and the shoulder she rode on shook as laughter spewed forth from both of them.

"What is so funny?" she demanded.

"No wonder he's feeling emasculated," chortled Lash. "Captured by a girl."

"No wonder he wants to punish you." Gunner shook his head. "You are in trouble, young lady. You chose the wrong fellow to mess with."

"So I'm discovering," she muttered.

The stairs they took down had a second entrance at the bottom, one that led directly outside. She could have yelled. Should have.

She didn't. *Why aren't I freaking out and letting Zola know?* Because she was curious.

Stupid.

Confused.

They bustled her into a golf cart, covering her with a tarp as they jounced down the roads leading to the dock. She didn't need to hear the caw of the gulls to know they'd reached their destination.

What surprised her was that Zola hadn't yet come to her rescue. What was she waiting for?

A chance to escape never presented itself. Despite the jovial humor of Gavin's buddies, they took their task seriously.

Which means I'm stuck waiting for whatever punishment Gavin intends to mete out. Because she didn't doubt he meant it. Asshole.

What form his revenge would take, though, remained to be seen. Would he rape her? Kill her?

Seduce her and prove just how weak she was around him?

Her newest captors sat her on the bunk and then took up positions against the opposite wall. She watched them through hooded eyes, waiting for a chance to escape, however they made effective guards and knew to keep themselves out of her reach.

The thud of footsteps on deck alerted her and she stiffened. She turned her head, pretending disinterest only catch her guards grinning at her.

She flipped to look the other way only to catch a glimpse of Gavin as he entered. Curse her damned heart for speeding up at the sight of him clad in low-hipped jean cutoffs and a t-shirt that did more to delineate his upper body than hide it.

While her body might tingle at his appearance, he spared not a single glance in her direction, choosing instead to murmur softly with his companions. Lash and Gunner left the cabin and a moment later the engine started and the boat began to move.

We're going out to sea. Not good for her. What did he plan to do? What she was certain was she wouldn't enjoy it.

I have to get away. But how? She couldn't hope to overpower three men and take over the ship, and she'd had time to realize that her last attempt to swim away had been beyond stupid.

Gavin settled himself at the tight table and chair, both bolted to the floor to prevent them crashing around in storms or tossing seas. He slapped a laptop on the surface and tapped at it, ignoring her.

It pricked her. While not a vain woman by nature, having a man—and not just any man but one who'd been inside her—ignoring her very existence irritated.

And hurt. She didn't understand why, but it did.

"Let me go." She tried the direct approach.

A pair of frigid eyes swiveled to peruse her. "No," he replied flatly, and turned away to continue tapping.

"Why are you doing this? I didn't hurt you."

"No, you used me."

"To—"

He cut her off. "To find your brother. I am aware of your reasoning. But your methods leave much to be desired."

"I'll do anything to help Ronin."

"That's obvious. Even stooping to whoring yourself. I have to wonder what your brother would think of that."

She ducked her head and replied in a low voice, "I didn't plan that."

"Then aren't I just the luckiest man. A pity you're a liar. Or have you so soon forgotten how I found you?"

"I wasn't planning to sleep with him."

"He seemed to think otherwise."

"He lied to me in order to get me to his room."

"Imagine that," was his dry reply. "How the hell you have survived this long is beyond my understanding."

"Ronin and Zola protected me." She was starting to realize just how much.

"They should have taught you how to survive without them." The disparagement stung, but not as much as the realization that he spoke the truth.

She was sheltered. Too sheltered, by men who didn't push when she said no. Who didn't look at her as a piece of meat. Family who respected her. Outside the compound, the blinders came off and she saw the reality in all its stark ugliness. And she hated it.

Anger boiled up inside her. "They did teach me how to survive," she spat, determined to defend them. "I know how to fight."

"Fighting should be your last resort. Do you even realize what kind of disadvantage you face?"

"I might be smaller—"

"Smaller?" Derisive laughter stuttered from him. "You're five feet of nothing. You probably weigh half of what I bench press, maybe less. No matter how good you are, in a battle of strength, you will lose each and every time."

"I know how to use a knife and shoot a gun."

"You can't always rely on those. And I saw how well your knife worked with Viper. If I hadn't come along, what would have happened?"

She preferred to not think on that. Just like she wanted to forget this entire conversation.

But he wouldn't let it go. "You are lucky I came looking for you because a few more minutes and you would have been raped. Maybe even dead. Viper isn't known for being gentle. It's why the brothels banned him."

"I didn't know that."

"You don't know a lot of things," he yelled.

From the set of his taut body, she could tell he seethed with anger, and yet she couldn't figure out why. Why did he care what happened to her?

"I guess I'm learning pretty fucking fast," she snarled back. "I realize I've made some mistakes." He snorted, but she ignored him and continued. "But I am doing my best."

"Your best isn't good enough."

"It has to be because if I don't try, then who knows what will happen to Ronin."

"You should leave the finding of your brother to those better suited for tracking."

"You mean a man." She glared at him. "That is sexist."

"Welcome to the real world, Ariel. This isn't America where everyone has equal rights. You and I don't live in the civilized parts of the Caribbean, we float among the edges, among the dregs. Laws don't apply to us. Genteel notions of equality of the sexes is a joke. You're an attractive woman. Too attractive. Everywhere you go, you draw attention. So far you've been running on luck. But that luck has ended."

"Because you're going to teach me a lesson," was her acerbic reply.

"Someone has to." His blue gaze bored into her.

"I don't need you lecturing."

"What a shame you don't have a choice. Kind of like the same way you gave me no choice when you tied me up and used my body."

"You enjoyed it."

"You didn't give me a choice!" he barked. "And what did you expect? I'm a man, and you're gorgeous. How the fuck was I supposed to say no when you were so fucking hot for me?"

A snicker made them both flash a glare at the door where Lash had popped his head in.

"What do you want?" Gavin snarled.

"Gunner and I were wondering what's for dinner."

"Get out." Gavin spoke the words softly, but Lash exited immediately, the door to the cabin not barrier enough to miss the explosive sound of his laughter.

"So this is about revenge," she noted, holding up her handcuffs.

"Did you think it was about anything else?"

Actually, when he'd come barging in to rescue her, yeah, she'd kind of hoped. Not that she'd admit it, not with this cold-eyed stranger.

"If you hurt me, Zola and Ronin will come after you and kill you," she promised.

He inclined his head toward her, and a dark smile tilted his lips. "They can try." With that veiled threat, he went back to ignoring her, head ducked as he tapped away again at his laptop.

It didn't sit well. Zola taught her many things: fighting—which worked best against smaller opponents not determined to hurt her—cooking—so she wouldn't starve the few times Zola left the compound for more than a few hours—and how to get blood out of clothes —a skill that saved many of Ronin's favorite shirts. But the most important thing Zola taught Steph was patience, which went hand in hand with controlling her temper, no matter the temptation or taunts.

In the face of Gavin's casual indifference, Steph forgot every damned thing she'd learned. Her patience burned away by rage and indignation—and pain, an odd ache that he truly hated her.

Without warning, she dove off the bunk and flew at him, hands still handcuffed, but she didn't care. She swung them like a club and missed as Gavin met her rush, rising from his seat. He caught her by the wrists and proved his point about strength.

Hands caught, she used her other body parts. She kicked and stomped. She landed several hits, some of which would surely leave some colorful bruises, but in the end, it was for naught.

He spun her around and held her tight against his length. She became all too aware of him. Her body tingled and she wasn't alone in being affected.

The hard ridge of his erection poked at her lower back. Moisture flooded her sex as she realized, despite his words, Gavin was still attracted to her.

His lips touched the lobe of her ear, the warmth of his breath sending a shiver coursing through her. "I don't have time for this."

He shoved her away from him, sending her stumbling. Hitting the edge of the bunk, she caught herself and turned.

To her disbelief, he pulled out a syringe from his back pocket. The clear vial was filled with fluid.

"Don't you dare," she spat. The idea of being incapacitated, at his mercy, both frightened and slammed home once again why he was so angry with her.

But regret at what she'd done didn't mean she'd let him casually drug her.

She charged at him, but he caught her one-armed.

She struggled in his grip. "Bastard. I'll kill you. You can't do this to me." Her head tilted back as she harangued him.

A tic pulsed in his cheek, but that didn't stop him from plunging the needle into her skin.

Sleepy time slammed in to her.

____

CHAPTER FOURTEEN

____

I'M AN ASSHOLE.

No getting around it. What guy drugged a woman?

The same one who went chasing after her because he wanted revenge. Revenge for making him come so hard, he thought he might die.

I have to find her.

To speed up his search for her, he'd commandeered Lash and Gunner, explaining simply, "Find this woman. She owes me."

She owed him for making him crazy.

It didn't help that the more time he spent away from her, the more he imagined her in the arms of another. Turned out he was right to fear. If he'd not gone to find Steph, she would right now be a broken or dead woman.

Some would say I did something heroic. And then he went and fucked it up by giving her a sleeping agent.

Better than knocking her out with a fist.

See, still kind of heroic. And by letting her snooze for a while, she'd have the strength for what came next.

Gavin caught her sagging body before it hit the floor.

Holding her fragile frame, anger coursed through him anew—a molten rage that demanded he embark on a murderous rampage—and it was all her fault.

What was she thinking, following Viper to his room?

If not for her companion, seated at a table, nursing a beer... "There you are. I wondered how long it would take you to come after her," said the woman with mahogany skin as he entered the bar. Without her, he wouldn't have even known Steph was in trouble.

"Where is she?" he'd growled, expecting to have to mete out some violence and threats to get the woman to talk.

"My dawta took her silly ass upstairs with some fellow. Not a nice fellow, I reckon," the woman had said.

How could she be so stupid?

How could she betray me? The surge of jealousy was unexpected, and it made his blood flow hot.

Livid didn't come close to describing his emotions when he burst into that room and saw another man touching her. A bastard who thought he could use his brute strength against her.

Against my Ariel!

Rage instantly washed over him and filled him to the point that he had to kill. Kill the man who tried to hurt her. Dared to touch her.

Just remembering the knot of fear in his stomach upon seeing her in Viper's grip made him want to kill the bastard again.

As he cradled her limp form in his arms, he couldn't help inhaling her scent, a sweet perfume of soap, nothing fancy, and yet it haunted his sleep—and even his waking moments.

You're mine, Ariel. The possessive thought had him tightening his grip on her.

He laid her on his bed, a bed sporting fresh sheets, washed in a failed attempt to pretend nothing happened.

I can't forget what you did to me, Ariel. Remembered it when he showered and his hand gripped his cock. Remembered it when he was in town and unable to evince any interest in those showcasing their sexual wares.

At the four corners of his bed were the same ropes she'd used to tie him down. As he tethered her, legs akimbo, ankles securely fastened, and her arms pulled taut over her head, he heard more than saw someone enter the cabin.

"You do realize she's probably like a buck twenty soaking wet?"

"And?" he absently replied.

"Don't you think the rope is overkill?" Gunner just had to offer his two cents.

"No one is asking you," Gavin said, frowning at the one knot on her ankle. He wanted her secured, not chafed. He loosened it.

"I didn't realize you were into kink," Lash added, joining the party.

Not usually. Gavin was a pretty straightforward kind of guy when it came to sex, but he'd planned this part of his revenge during their time apart—fantasized about it in fact. "She's too dangerous to leave loose."

Snort. "Yeah, so dangerous. Kind of like a cute little kitty that spits and claws but doesn't really leave a mark."

How little Gunner knew. She'd managed to leave an indelible mark. Gavin planned to return the favor.

"Are we gonna get to take turns?" Lash asked.

"Don't you fucking touch her!" Without even looking, Gavin donkey kicked, snapping his foot into Lash's leg, making him crumple.

"Ow! Totally uncalled for."

Gavin turned an icy gaze on to his two friends, his resolve sharper than any knife. "Let's get something clear. I don't want either of you anywhere near her. You are not to talk to her or touch."

"Can we breathe?" was Lash's sarcastic reply.

"No."

"What are you going to do with her?" Gunner asked, his glance straying to her limp form.

Sidestepping, Gavin blocked his view. "What I do with her is none of your fucking business." His gaze stroked over her, noticing how small and helpless she appeared in his bed. The ropes provided a visually crude symbol of his vengeance.

He turned away and caught the disapproving stare of his comrades.

"Don't give me that look."

"I'm not cool with you abusing women," Lash said, crossing his arms over his chest. "It's one thing to play Blackbeard and abduct them for ransom, but I won't stand by and watch you intentionally hurt one."

"I won't hurt her." In a bad way, but she might scream.

"Maybe you should let her go. Let her off at the next island with me and Lash."

Why was Gunner trying to take her from him?

In a flash, Gavin pinned the man against the wall,

the honed edge of his blade pressed against his neck. "She stays with me," he growled. "Do you hear me? She's mine, goddammit," Gavin shouted, stunning himself with his vehemence.

"We hear you loud and clear." Gunner stupidly didn't show as much fear as he should have given a dagger sat only a nudge away from slitting his throat.

The ramifications of his actions suddenly hit him. *What is wrong with me?* He'd never behaved like this about a woman before.

Gavin released Gunner and stepped away, yet didn't sheath his blade. Someone still wore too many clothes. Steph should taste what it felt like to wake naked and vulnerable, unable to do a thing about it.

"Get out," he told his friends because the next part of his plan shouldn't have an audience. The visual prize of her body was his and his alone. Gavin wasn't about to share it with others.

"Promise you're not going to kill her," Gunner demanded.

"Or cut her up," Lash added.

"I'm not going to hurt her." Why kill her when revenge would taste much sweeter? Feel so climatic. "But I might start maiming you both if you don't move your asses."

With a shared look and a shrug, his friends left, shutting the door behind them. Silence reigned in the cabin except for the soft sound of her breathing.

Alone again, Gavin turned and looked down upon her, the way her lashes touched the very tops of her cheeks. How her full mouth parted slightly with each breath, and her tits rose and fell with each inhalation.

So vulnerable. But not exposed enough.

He went to work, slicing through her clothes, denuding her. Despite having seen and tasted her before, the sight still managed to hitch his breath and give him an instant erection.

As fabric parted, he couldn't help drawing a finger down the soft valley between her breasts. This was the first time he truly got to touch her. And she was silky.

He let his fingers circle around her tits before he drew them to her nipple. It immediately puckered at his touch. He tugged on her dusky aureoles, and could easily imagine himself pulling on them as she rode him, her fiery red hair a silken curtain bouncing down her back.

He couldn't resist torqueing the tip. Even asleep, her body responded to him, her nipples hard, her body shivering, and a peek between her legs at the pink shell of her cunt showed it glistening. Wet.

His prick hardened and his balls drew tight with desire. He'd still yet to figure out why she attracted him so much.

His fingers continued their exploration. The fiery thatch at the apex of her thighs called. He slid his fingers through her curls to her damp sex.

As he parted her nether lips, she quivered, and a soft sigh signaled her approach to wakefulness. He hadn't given her a strong dose of the drugs. Just enough to quiet her while he got her ready.

He stroked her again, the moisture of her cunt coating his finger, slick honey begging for a taste. He almost bent over before realizing she was seducing him again, and this time, it was his own fault.

As if burned, he stepped away from her just as her lashes fluttered open.

"I'm not dead," she murmured, sounding surprised.

The fact she thought him capable—*I totally am*—made him bristle, and so he replied tersely, "Death is too quick. I told you, I intend to give you tit for tat."

A sigh escaped her, one of irritation. "My torture was for answers. What am I supposed to give you?"

Your heart?

He almost punched himself for the sissy thought. Despite his envy of Cole, he wasn't truly looking for a woman to settle down with.

Am I?

"I'm sure you have some secrets to tell," he growled.

"I know the ingredients to Zola's special roti's. Speaking of whom, you didn't hurt her, did you?"

"Who is Zola?"

"My foster mom. She was with me in the bar."

"If you mean the woman with dreadlocks and that smiley face t-shirt with a bullet hole, then yeah, I met her."

"What did you do with her?" She tried to lift herself on the bed, but the rope did its trick.

"What makes you think I did anything?"

"Because she wouldn't have let that man hurt me. She always protects me. Which means someone stopped her."

"I didn't do shit to her. Last I saw, she was still drinking in the bar. She didn't seem too concerned about you at all." He lied.

And she knew it. "Bullshit."

"If she's so protective of you, then how come she left you alone with me before?"

"You were tied up at the time. And she came back

once you weren't." Her lips curved into a smile. "Or have you so soon forgotten the lump on your head?"

He grimaced. "I'm more annoyed she got the drop on me." Then again, he was distracted. "That won't happen again."

"What did you do to her?" she yelled, misconstruing his words."

"Nothing."

"Swear it."

"No need to swear shit because I don't hurt women."

"And yet, here I am, tied to your bed." She tugged at her tethers.

"Just repaying the favor."

"So tit for tat is it?" She arched a brow. "Good to know I just need to tolerate you for a day or so before you let me go."

Never. You are mine. The words rose unbidden in his mind, almost slipped off his lips. "You'll leave when I say you can leave. It might be a day, two, or a month. Depends on my mood."

"Asshole."

"I've been called worse."

"Since you're being totally unreasonable—"

"Says the woman who kidnapped me."

"—then why don't you get started? Do your worst." Her expression dared him.

As a man, he felt compelled to act. "What's the first thing you did to me?" He pretended to think, tapping his chin. "I remember. Do you?" He grinned, and he saw her swallow hard. "You slapped me in the balls." He looked down at her exposed cunt. "No balls to hit there. I guess I'll have to improvise."

Before he could talk himself out of it, he slapped her tit. A fleshy smack to each one that had them jiggling.

She glared. "Seriously?"

"This is kind of fun." And just because he was in the mood, he slapped her breast again.

Angry as she might try to be, she couldn't hide the flush in her skin or how her heart rate increased.

She wants me.

For some reason, he'd wondered. He still couldn't figure out why she'd chosen him to take her virginity. *Why me?* An attractive girl like her didn't save herself only to give it away to a stranger. Was it possible she suffered the same insane attraction as him?

Only one way to find out.

He leaned over, his lips hovering above hers, a luscious temptation he couldn't resist. He kissed her, pressing his mouth hard against hers in a fierce brand, that of a man claiming his woman.

She didn't protest. Not by words, or by turning away. On the contrary, her mouth parted and small hums of pleasure escaped her.

He slid his tongue past the barrier of her lips, tasting her sweetness, and groaning when she hesitantly let her own tongue touch him back. The innocence in her caress undid him.

Climbing on to the bunk, he covered her nude body with his own, nestling his bigger frame between her thighs. His rigid cock, even behind the material of his jeans, pressed against her cunt. He couldn't help but give it a rub and she gasped in his mouth. Her hips pushed against him, a silent plea for more.

And he intended to give it to her, to sink himself into her silky body and fuck her until she screamed his name, *my name,* as she climaxed on his cock and he planted his seed inside her.

Like a cold shower, the thought of babies froze him. He stopped and lifted his head.

"Ariel, are you on the pill?"

Heavy-lidded eyes opened to peek at him. "The what?"

"Pill as in birth control." Even before she replied no, he saw the answer.

With a curse, he rolled off her and stalked out of the cabin, away from temptation. Hitting the deck, he made his way to the rail and clutched it, head dropped, an ocean breeze ruffling his hair. He stared without seeing at the slice of his yacht through the water.

Thoughts tumbled through his mind, first and foremost, the woman in his cabin could be pregnant.

With my child.

The idea should have horrified him. Sent him speeding to the nearest island pharmacy for one of those pills women took to ensure it didn't take root.

But did he tell his friends to change course?

Did he panic at the thought of her belly rounding with a child?

My child.

Nope. He wanted to march back in there and fuck her. Fuck her over and over and over until he made damn sure he'd planted something in her belly.

What is wrong with me? He barely knew her. Wasn't even sure he wanted to be a father.

Tossing a ball on the beach.

Riding the child around on my shoulders as they laugh.

He shut his eyes against the memories of the childhood he never got, but wanted to give.

Would I even make a good father?

Not happening. He wasn't daddy or husband material. He was a smuggler, a killer, a guy working for a criminal organization, although Henderson would probably object to him calling it that.

We deal in exports and imports of delicate goods. That sometimes required a little law breaking and bloodshed. It wasn't a career that was conducive to starting a family.

What was he thinking? No one wanted to settle down with one woman forever. Was it Lash who said variety is the pussy of life? He most definitely didn't need kids in it, needy little things that spent their time eating, shitting, or screaming.

Calling me Daddy and holding up their arms for a hug.

Shoot me now. He didn't want it. Swore he'd never settle down with a woman after Sasha fucked him over, spreading her thighs for anyone with a shiny bauble. The woman who managed to drive a wedge between him and his best friend.

Steph's different.

She didn't whore herself out for money. She was pure and sweet and brave. Stupidly brave. What idiot with no life skills went looking for her brother among the dregs of society?

One who cared.

Cared about her brother. Not Gavin.

Gunner and Lash were right. He should cut her loose. Drop her off at the next island and return to his regular life.

I can't.

I won't.

Apparently that Zola broad must have whacked him pretty hard in the head and scrambled what few wits he had left because he wasn't about to set Steph free. Not yet. Not while his body burned for her.

Could it be that simple? Could he fuck his way to curing his obsession?

Or will having sex only make it worse?

Only one way to find out. It was with firm purpose that he went stalking back to the cabin.

Upon his entry, he caught her wary gaze.

"If it isn't the pussy teaser," she said with a frown.

"What's wrong, Ariel? Is the torture getting to you already? Going to beg me for more."

"I don't need you."

"Are you sure? Are you going to tell me you haven't imagined my mouth sucking on your tits? Did you know I dreamed about it? But you never did let me get a taste."

"You're sick."

"And you're horny." The evidence was in the way her nipples pulled into tight buds.

"It's cold."

"I know how to warm you up." His words emerged gruff.

She snorted. "Don't bother. I'm fine."

"But I insist." Knowing she watched, he took his time as he stripped, even folding his clothes before placing them on a chair.

"I don't want this."

"Are you sure about that? I'll bet if I touch your cunt, it's wet."

"Maybe I peed myself."

He laughed. "Oh, Ariel. We both know that's a lie.

And I've finally figured out what I want you to tell me." He leaned over her and plucked a ripe nipple. "Tell me you want me."

"Never."

He ran his hand up her leg, noting the tremble of her limb as he traveled up, closer and closer to her core. "Tell me you want me to fuck you."

"I'd rather go back to sleep," she replied, somewhat breathlessly.

"There will be no sleep for you tonight, Ariel," he murmured as he leaned down to press his lips against the creamy skin of her thigh. A quiver ran through her and he held in a smile as he brushed soft kisses on her leg. "Tell me," he whispered as he moved close enough to her cunt to smell her arousal. "Admit you want to feel my tongue lashing your clit. Tell me how you want to come on my tongue."

"I don't." The words but a breathless whisper.

"You're lying." He nuzzled the soft fuzz at her pelvis and heard her suck in a breath.

"I don't want you."

The fact she so blatantly lied when the truth of her arousal perfumed the very air made him angry.

"If I recall, the next step of your torture involved a certain position. Shall we recap?" He had to carefully maneuver to get himself in a proper 69 position, his knees cradling the top of her head, his mouth hovering over her sex.

This time, she had no smartass reply. Then again, what could she say once he lowered his cock and pressed it against her lips?

This could have gone badly at this point. Sharp

teeth could do damage. But he'd judged her correctly, her need for him stronger.

Her mouth opened wide to take him and she began to suck. Suck him hard. Suck him thoroughly and he closed his eyes, basking in the bliss.

Pleasure, though, should always go two ways.

He lowered his head between her thighs and dipped his tongue for a long lick across her wet cunt. Then winced as her mouth clamped down on his cock. Her hips thrust upward, knocking him in the chin.

A violent and yet satisfying reaction.

He placed his arms across her thighs, anchoring her, before he dove in again for another lick. Back and forth, he swiped his tongue while she squirmed and gasped, the sound vibrating on his cock. He parted the lips of her sex and lapped at her, tasting her cream, feeling her flesh pulsing against his tongue.

Eventually, he moved on to her clit, that swollen pleasure button that only took a few strokes and one firm pull of his lips to make her come with a scream. A scream that almost made him shoot his load in her mouth.

But then that would mean not sinking in to the velvety glove of her sex.

Repositioning himself between her legs, he stared down at her. She was so fucking gorgeous, her lips parted, her skin flushed, and her eyes closed as she basked in the aftershocks of her orgasm.

Time to give her another.

Placing his palms under her ass, he hoisted her upwards, high enough to bring her level with his bobbing cock. He nudged her cunt, parting the wet lips with his swollen head. He got to watch and enjoy as his prick slid into her pinkness. A drawn out moan escaped her. He glanced at her face and saw her staring at him through heavy-lidded eyes.

Locking gazes, he fucked her, his cock sliding into her welcoming sheath and retreating. The tight suction of her cunt indescribable.

In and out, he thrust in to her, flesh slapping against flesh, each long stroke drawing mewling cries from her.

Keeping up his pace, he folded himself against her, his mouth hotly seeking. They kissed while he pistoned, her hips lifting to meet his thrusts, her sweet cunt tightening and fisting his cock until he couldn't hold back any longer.

He yelled as he came, his seed shooting from him, triggering her orgasm. The muscles of her sex locked around his cock, holding him deep inside.

And he was okay with that.

In the aftermath, as their bodies cooled, he pressed soft kisses on her temple, cheeks, the corner of her mouth.

She was so soft in that moment. So vulnerable. He almost forgot his plan. Almost let her go.

To fight the urge, he said, "Tell me you want me."

When she told him to fuck off, they started over again.

CHAPTER FIFTEEN

A NORMAL REACTION TO BEING TIED UP AND SEDUCED over and over again would be ranting and raving and hating the man holding her body prisoner. Instead of trying to catch her breath at the decadent pleasures he inflicted on her, Steph should have plotted ways of escaping.

She didn't.

The expected anger at her situation never truly materialized. The frustration at her inability to free herself turned into pleasure, the woman in her titillated by the fact she was at his mercy, a captive to his erotic torture.

Even worse, from what she knew, her extreme reaction to him wasn't the norm. It was Gavin who made her feel this way. Gavin she wanted.

And yet, she knew he wouldn't care. Once he tired of her, she'd get the boot. Or the plank. No matter his method, once he'd had his fill of her body, and tired of revenge, she'd be sent on her way.

The realization deflated her. The ache in her chest

told her she didn't want to lose him. In the short time they'd known each other, she'd found someone who intrigued her, who made her feel things, and it went beyond incredible sex. She wanted to know more about him, who he was and where he came from. What were his likes and dislikes?

I want a relationship. A foolish dream that could never be.

"Why do you look sad?" His question snapped her back to the present and she looked up to see him staring at her. For once, his face didn't appear angry or bear an indifferent mask.

Tell him you like him. He'd probably mock her. It sounded dorky even admitting it to herself. So, she opted for a half truth. "This might sound weird, but I'm gonna miss the screwing when I'm gone."

The soft look on Gavin's face was overtaken by a glare. "You're not leaving."

"You can't keep me on your boat forever." Even if it sounded divine.

"Yes, I can."

"You'll have to untie me eventually. Or were you planning on getting me a bedpan?" She arched a brow.

"Even if I did untie you, there's nowhere to run when we're at sea."

"What's your plan then? Keep me a prisoner forever?" Her heart thumped, hoping he'd say yes.

Instead, he rolled off her and paced, his naked body a thing of beauty to watch. Even though they'd just had sex, arousal stirred.

"I'm not letting you go," he muttered darkly.

"You can't watch me forever. When I get a chance, I will go." *Unless you ask me to stay.*

The very idea shocked her, and so she missed his sudden movement. He was suddenly atop of her, the heat of his naked flesh a delightful friction.

"You're staying with me," he snarled. His mouth found hers in a bruising kiss that left no room for thought, only pleasure.

His hands, callused and rough, roamed her flesh, making her aware of her body in ways she'd never imagined. With his mouth, he drew tortured cries from her, blissful sounds that encouraged him to give her more, and more, until she thought she would die from sheer delight.

What a way to go.

Don't ever let me go.

CHAPTER SIXTEEN

As Gavin slid from the bed, and the warm curve of Steph's body, he couldn't help but feel tense. A dark brooding invaded him.

The ropes binding her bothered him. Yet, she'd made it clear she would escape if he didn't keep her tied.

At the same time, he recalled the soreness of his own limbs during his captivity.

I don't want to hurt her.

Lips pressed in a tight line, he grabbed his knife from the table and sliced the bonds. She didn't wake, but immediately noticed the lessening pressure and turned on her side. He drew a sheet over her nude body, the gesture gentle and unlike him. So many things he'd done since meeting her were unlike him.

Restless, he exited the cabin and ran into Lash. Not many places to hide on his small yacht. Good thing they'd hit land soon.

"After all the yelling, I expected you to wear a smile," Lash said. "Or at least walk bow-legged."

Gavin didn't have the capacity to be embarrassed that someone heard them. But Lash better watch his mouth. "Do you have something important to say, or are you just here to piss me off and waste air?"

"Just making conversation."

Gavin arched a brow.

Lash laughed as he leaned against the rail. "You are awfully prickly, and given your mood, I'm probably gonna regret asking this, but what's the plan?"

"I'll be dropping you off in the morning like we discussed."

'And the girl?"

"Is still none of your business."

"Are you sure you don't want to drop her at the same time? You know what they say about chicks and ships. Bad luck, man."

"I can handle one woman."

"Can you? I've never seen you act like this before."

"Like what?" Gavin asked.

"As if you might have a thing for the broad. Which is crazy. Single, swinging Gavin would never settle down with one woman."

"You're right I wouldn't." *Unless she was perfect for me.*

"So, you're not serious about her then? This is just about sex?"

A shrug lifted Gavin's shoulders. "Sex and revenge. Nothing more." He couldn't admit it was something more. Not yet. Maybe not ever.

"How long are you going to punish her?"

Forever. He would never tire of her screams and sighs of pleasure. "Why do you fucking care?" He couldn't prevent the vehement query.

"I care because I think you are falling for the girl."

"Like hell. She's just a good fuck."

"She means nothing?"

"Not a thing."

"So, if I were to go down there and ogle her naked body, maybe slap her fine ass—"

Gavin didn't even know he'd moved until Lash went overboard and hit the water with a splash.

The big fellow immediately bobbed to the surface with a laugh. "Way to prove my point. You like a girl!" Lash sang.

With a snort of disgust, Gavin tossed a life ring to the man, one with the rope tethered to the boat, and then stomped to the wheelhouse where he ignored Gunner at the wheel. He pulled out a hidden bottle of rum and tipped it. The alcohol heated its way to his stomach.

His back to him, Gunner said in a low tone, "It's not the end of the world if you like this chick." Sound carried at sea, which made it impossible to have secrets.

"Except she doesn't like me. She only ever fucked me to get information about her brother. And the worst part is, she thought I was someone else when she did," Gavin replied. Did it mean she would have fucked anyone to get what she wanted?

The virgin factor said no, but her desperation to find her brother...confused the hell out of him

"What I heard had nothing to do with finding anyone."

"Maybe she's faking it. Or has an ulterior motive."

"I know where you're going with this again. And don't you even start." Gunner shot him a glare over his shoulder. "We all told you Sasha was a slut, but you wouldn't listen. How many years did you stop talking to Cole because of her bullshit?"

"This has nothing to do with my ex." And yet it did. Sasha broke him. Broke his trust. Ariel hadn't yet done that, however she made no bones about the fact she was using Gavin to find her brother. And when she did? She'd leave.

Sudden frustration and anger made him fling the bottle, only Gunner caught it before it could smash. He took a swig and smacked his lips. "Thanks for sharing. Now for some advice. Stop being a dick."

"Kind of hard given the size of the one between my legs."

"You know what I mean, numbnut. You like this girl, and judging by her 'oh Gavins,' she likes you, too. Stop being a dumbass and try treating her like a lady."

"You mean bow and scrape like a pussy," Gavin growled.

"Don't you growl at me when I'm giving you good advice. Being nice to her isn't weak or emasculating. It's called respecting your lady."

"What if she doesn't want to be my lady?"

Gunner's brow arched. "Are you seriously going to be a coward about this? I know you're a fighter. Since when do you give in so easily? You want this woman?"

"Yeah."

"You like this woman?"

"Yeah." The admission finally slipped past his lips.

"Then untie the girl, and be nice."

"I already did, but you do know once we hit port, she's gonna leave me to find her brother."

"So, be her fucking hero and find him first."

The simplicity of the plan stunned him. "How the fuck am I supposed to do that?"

"Well for starters, you said she thought you were someone else."

"Yeah. The real Crusty Seadog."

"Lucky for you, I know where he is and we're already going there. Although, I might advise you to take the long route."

"Why the long path?"

A loud sigh escaped Gunner. "For a smartass, you're awfully dense sometimes. The longer you keep her, the more likely she is to fall for your ugly mug and want to stay. Maybe if you stopped hiding your head up your ass, you'd realize that keeping her tied up as your sex slave when she's worried about her brother might not be the best course of action."

"But she looks good naked and spread eagle," Gavin replied with a grin. *So very fucking good.*

"I'll bet she does. But, imagine the things you could do together if she wasn't tied up."

Doggy style came to mind. Dammit. "Since when do you say intelligent things?"

"Since saying smart shit gets me laid," Gunner joked. "Now if you'll excuse me, I need to fish Lash out of the drink. The idiot is just bobbing along in his life ring. Meanwhile, I'm pretty sure that's a shark, not a dolphin following him."

Gunner left while Gavin sat there in pensive silence, rolling over in his mind the things Gunner had said, most of which made sense.

He did like Steph, not that he planned to tell her anytime soon. A man didn't give that kind of ammo to a woman. The realization that he did want to spend more time with her, and not just in bed, surprised and excited him.

Who was she? What made her tick? Why was her bond to her brother so strong? Then came the trickier questions. *Can I make her like me? Convince her to stay. Maybe even love me.*

Love.

Fuck. Was he ready to take that plunge again?

Then again, it would only work if he could win her over, and there was only one way to assure that.

I have to find her brother.

CHAPTER SEVENTEEN

WAKING UP TO THE SLANTING RAYS OF SUNLIGHT
filtering through a blind, Steph snuggled into the pillow
cradling her head, hands tucked under her cheek, lulled
by the gentle rocking of a boat.

The simple act made one thing clear.

I'm not tied up.

The whole kidnapping by Gavin, the tit for tat
abduction and seduction, must have been a dream. An
erotic fantasy that came about because she pined after
the man she'd kidnapped and lost.

It made logical sense, except her tiny bed aboard the
ship with Zola was never this comfortable, and the smell
was all wrong.

Because I'm not on our ship!

Her eyes popped open and she noted a familiar
cabin. *His* cabin. Yet, she clearly recalled being tied
spread eagle when she passed out after the epic sex. Not
anymore.

Sitting up, the blanket fell to her waist. No one
appeared to be in the room with her, and the bathroom

door gaped open. She ignored the pang of disappointment that Gavin was nowhere to be seen. Probably for the best. She couldn't seem to control herself around the man.

Then again, he had the same difficulty, too. He was insatiable. Or did it just seem that way to a woman with almost no experience?

She wished she had Zola to ask. Then again, Zola had thrown her to the mercenary. No way had Gavin managed to steal her without Zola noticing.

Was her foster mother playing matchmaker? How out of character. Then again, Steph knew Zola wanted something for her dawta other than a gang life. *Does Zola secretly want to be a grandmother?* Or was she just determined to ensure her daughter experienced pleasure and love?

Love?

Her nose wrinkled. She didn't love Gavin. Not one bit. The man meant nothing to her. He wasn't even a means to the end anymore, seeing as how he knew nothing about Ronin.

Which reminded her. What happened to the matchbook she'd stashed in her bra? She'd woken naked. But what of the clue she'd almost paid dearly for?

She stretched as she climbed out of the bed, her joints popping and cracking. Despite her being tied for hours, and the numerous times Gavin made her body sing, she felt great. Better than great, actually.

And hungry. Her rumbling stomach protested, as did her bladder.

She quickly took care of the one issue, even managing a rapid sluice in his small stall, the water tepid but refreshing. She then padded barefoot to the door of the cabin. She didn't actually want to exit, not naked, but she was curious. No surprise, the door didn't open at her tug.

Apparently, while Gavin no longer felt a need to have her tied up, he didn't trust her to roam his ship. He'd also not left anything she could use as a weapon, although she could probably do some damage with the toothbrush she found. However, she wasn't about to start a fight. Not until she knew why he'd set her free.

Did this mean he'd finished his revenge? Would he be setting her ashore at his next stop?

While she rummaged for a weapon, she found some oversized t-shirts bearing his scent. She could have worn one, covered her nudity, but chose not to. Perhaps she could use her nakedness to gain an advantage.

Maybe he'll be so overcome with lust he'll pounce me and make me scream again.

Shiver. She should be so lucky.

With nothing to do, she sat on the bed, lotus style. Closing her eyes, she attempted to relax and drop into a meditative state, something Zola tried in vain to teach her. Steph was more interested in learning to bend her body than breathe in through her nose and out through her mouth.

But she tried, needing some kind of relief to the turmoil in her mind. All the blank slate did was enable her to more vividly picture the things she'd done with Gavin. More like the things he did to her. Pleasurable acts.

He was right. He can do so much more when he's not tied up. Her body flushed and her breasts felt heavy, the nipples hardening.

As if her arousal acted as a signal, the door opened. Eyes closed, Steph held still, pretending indifference.

For all she knew, it was Lash or Gunner. However, given how her body reacted, and how the very air seemed charged with anticipation, she suspected it was Gavin. Only for him did her nipples pout for attention. Only for Gavin did her pussy get so wet.

Something hit her in the face and her eyes flew open as silken fabric tumbled into her lap.

"What the hell?" she snapped just before all the air sucked from her lungs. Gavin's fault for looking sexier than a pirate, his leather pants skin tight, his white shirt open halfway down his chest. He'd not shaved in a few days—her thighs tingled remembering the rough rub of his whiskers. He wore a hoop in one ear, eyeliner around his eyes, and a wicked smile.

"Is it Jack Sparrow day?" she asked with an arched brow.

"Of a sorts. Get dressed," he ordered, his voice gruff.

Holding up the material on her lap, her brow creased as she tried to make sense of the filmy fabric. "What is this supposed to be?"

"A dress."

"I think it's missing parts."

"It's supposed to. You need to look like a prostitute."

It didn't take any thought. She flung the clothes at him with a tart, "Like hell."

He caught the piss poor excuse for a dress and stalked toward her. A predatory strut that only increased her desire for him.

How dare he look so damned sexy!

Refusing to be distracted by his tempting body,

Steph scrambled off the bed and faced him, fists clenched.

"You will wear this."

"Not in this lifetime."

"Either you put it on, or I will."

"Go ahead and wear it. I think it's your color."

His lips flattened. "You know what I mean. Put this dress on or I will manhandle your ass into it."

The imp in her had her replying with a sassy, "I'd like to see you try."

"You'll do as I say," he stated with cocky assurance.

"Not today. Not ever. I'm not your slave. I don't have to listen to you."

"You will obey!" He said it firmly.

She didn't care. "I don't have to do shit for you."

"Why must you be so stubborn?" he yelled.

"Why are you such a dick?" she hollered back. "I understand you're still pissed at what I did, but that doesn't mean you get the right to order me around."

"I'm trying to help you."

"By dressing me like a whore? What's the point? You've already seen the goods." She thrust out her chest.

His eyes flickered, the hunger in them clear, and yet he didn't make a grab for her. What exactly was he up to?

"We don't have time for this."

"Maybe you don't have time, but I'm in the mood." The fight totally had her blood and other things running hot. "If you're not capable of satisfying me, then maybe we should call in your friends to help out."

The stillness of his body should have warned her she'd gone too far, but it still took her by surprise when he leaped. His larger body slammed into hers and pushed her against the bunk. Before she could even assemble her wits enough to fight, he'd grasped each of her hands and yanked them over her head, effectively trapping her.

Desire raced through her body, igniting all her nerve endings, flooding her pussy with moisture.

"You are to stay away from Gunner and Lash unless you'd like to be the reason I kill them," he growled. The threat brushed over her lips, vibrating with anger—and passion.

"Why do you care who I sleep with? I'm nothing to you."

"You're mine right now. Mine alone to touch and tease." He pressed himself against her, the hardness of his erection evident.

"What if I don't want you?"

"Liar." His lips brushed over hers, stealing her breath, stuttering the rapid beat of her heart. "I can see your lust. Smell it. And if we had time, I'd taste it and prove you wrong. But it will have to wait." He pushed away from her, body still taut with the anger simmering beneath the surface.

"I hate you." She expected anger or retaliation at her inflammatory statement.

Instead, he laughed. "No you don't. Like me, you want to fight what's happening between us. Pretend it's not a tsunami threatening to overtake us. But in the end, I suspect we will both be swept away."

"What are you saying?" Because it sounded as if... no. She was reading too much into it.

"Later, Ariel. Get dressed."

Crossing her arms over her chest, she shook her head. "I'll wear my own clothes, thank you, not some slut's cast-offs." Whose dress was this? Girlfriend? Lover? Someone she could dispose of and leave no one the wiser? "And while you're at it, I need the matchbook that was in my bra."

"Since when do you smoke?"

"I don't. I got it from Viper before he turned all rapey on me."

"The only clothes you had I sliced from you and tossed."

"And the matches?"

He shrugged. "Gone too."

"You bastard. It had the name of the place my brother was last seen in."

"You are assuming Viper told you the truth."

"And if he was?" she snarled. "Now I have nothing."

"Which is why you should get dressed, unless you'd prefer to go ashore naked?"

The hip she cocked made a great place for her hand. She also thrust her chest forward. "Why cover it up? Or are you saying you don't like what you see?" Now she was being deliberately stubborn. Mostly because the mention of docking and going ashore brought on a moment of panic. *He's getting rid of me.*

It was too soon.

Wait, this was what she wanted. Ronin needed her.

I need Gavin.

He reminded her of a predator on the prowl as he stalked toward her with slow, fluid movements. Super sexy. Also kind of scary. Mostly because she didn't know what he wanted from her. Everything was so confusing.

He stopped in front of her, not touching, yet the heat of him radiated. "You are driving me nuts."

"Says the pirate," she retorted.

"Mercenary, actually. Sometimes smuggler. And a man who isn't used to having women talk back."

"That must be a change from 'oh, Gavin, you're so wonderful. Let me drop my panties for you.'"

His lips twitched. "And yet again, another example of that filthy mouth of yours."

"Which, let me guess, is best suited for sucking your dick?"

"You do have a perfect mouth for it." His lids shuttered his eyes, adopting the smoky expression she'd come to know indicated he was aroused.

"What do you want from me?" she asked. From the moment he'd entered the cabin, she got the sense something had changed between them, but she couldn't pinpoint what.

"I want you to put on the damned dress so we can go ashore."

"Then what?"

"Why not put it on and see?"

"I don't like surprises."

"Are you sure about that? Because I assure you, this is one you won't want to miss. I will give you a hint. It has to do with your brother."

Ronin? "You found something?"

"Perhaps. But I will warn you right now, it is a slim clue, possibly nothing. We can explore it together, or—since you seem so inclined to tempt me—we could remain here and fuck the day away until the next tide."

The thought of him touching her and then driving in to her with his thick cock did all kinds of decadent things to her body. But…pleasure had to come second to her brother.

"Let's go check out this clue." With a moue of

distaste, she put on the outfit as he leaned against the wall, watching with a seemingly negligent air.

Once dressed, she looked down at herself and grimaced. "I look cheap."

"I would have said delicious." His voice was husky.

It startled her, and she noted the hunger in his expression. Someone liked the short filmy skirt that barely covered her ass and pussy. The silky top was more like two fabric strips that rose to cover her breasts, the material molding to them, delineating her nipples. There was a deep vee between the swathes that tied around her neck, leaving her entire back bare.

She bent over—flashing her ass on purpose—and put on her sandals, the only thing he'd saved.

"Fuck me!" he cursed.

Straightening, she noted his frown. "What's wrong?" Did she look stupid in it?

"What's wrong is I'd rather not have to kill people as soon as we set foot on the dock. You'll have to change."

It took her a second to grasp his problem with the outfit. "You think I'm too sexy?" She couldn't help a pleased smile.

"Every man who sees you is going to want to lift that skirt and fuck that sweet cunt of yours."

She smiled. "And that's a bad thing?"

"It might be. I'd rather not fight off a bunch of assholes who think you're available for taking."

"I can protect myself."

He reached out and grabbed her by the back of the neck, yanking her close. "I'll protect you. Never doubt that." He crushed his mouth to hers, the kiss long and deep and tingling.

When it stopped, she couldn't help but let out a mewl of disappointment.

He groaned. "Don't make this harder than it has to be."

Boldly, she cupped the front of him and whispered in a low voice, "Already feels hard to me."

"Dammit, Ariel."

She laughed, heady with this new power she'd found. The power of sex and seduction.

Heading to the door of the cabin, she tossed a coy look over her shoulder at Gavin. "Are you *coming?*"

The sound he made was deeply satisfying.

She skipped out onto the deck and noted they were docked, the pier they bobbed at busy with ships of all sizes, from schooners with sails tied down tight, to sleek yachts bigger than Gavin's. Other piers in the bay held fishing vessels of all sizes. What she didn't spot was the familiar blue hull of Zola's boat. Then again, this place was huge. It could easily be hidden amongst them.

And do I really want Zola to come to my rescue? Not right now. Perhaps not ever.

The slight breeze on deck ruffled the short hem on her skirt. Despite her brave words below deck, out here in the open she felt exposed. Almost naked. She also couldn't help but notice the eyes watching her. The leers aimed in her direction as men nearby stopped what they were doing to stare.

She felt Gavin arrive behind her, a solid presence at her back, emanating menace. "I should have locked you below deck and done this on my own," he said in a low murmur.

"How about giving me a knife or something to protect myself?"

"And risk you gutting me?"

"If I wanted to gut you, I would have used the fork I found in the cupboard by the coffee maker."

"Death by forking." He snickered. "That almost sounds dirty."

"Only because you're a man."

"That's right. I am, and you're going to have to trust me to protect you, because where we're going, women aren't allowed to have weapons. It's scares off the clients."

"Where exactly are we going?" she asked as he hopped onto the pier and then turned to hold out his arms to her.

He caught her in them and murmured, "We're going to visit the local whorehouse."

<hr>

CHAPTER EIGHTEEN

<hr>

GAVIN PROBABLY DESERVED SOME OF THE CHOICE names Steph muttered under her breath. Especially since, at first, she mistakenly assumed he was trying to sell her services.

As if he'd let anyone touch her.

It took a hard kiss, one that claimed her in full view of everyone watching, and a whisper that the whorehouse was the one on the matchbook he'd thrown out, for her to calm down.

Pity his nerves weren't so easily tamed. The outfit she wore, fetched earlier that day when he sent idiots one and two ashore, was perfect for their mission, and at the same time the most heinous garment ever. The damned thing did too good of a job showcasing her luscious body.

A body that men ogled.

Not usually a jealous man by nature, Gavin found himself taut and simmering as he noted all the stares directed her way. If he had the time, he might have taken care of a few. As it was, he suspected he'd have to indulge in a fight or two just to prove a point. *She's mine.*

If you think that, then why not say it? Tell her.

Admit it out loud? That posed a few problems. The first being rejection. He wasn't sure how he'd handle it. When he'd found out his girlfriend cheated on him in his youth, he'd embarked on a downward spiral, pushing away his friends and drinking himself into a stupor.

Older, not any wiser, but definitely more violent, would her rejection or ridicule send him spiraling like it had when he was a younger man?

He couldn't answer for sure. Just like he couldn't spout flowery platitudes or simpering speeches about how he thought she was the most awesome thing since butter basted scallops—and those were pretty fucking delicious. Just not as delicious as Steph.

Since when did he need fancy fucking words? Usually, he crooked a finger, dropped a nugget of gold, or flashed a smile, and chicks were all over him. While Steph might have initially seduced him, she now fought their mutual attraction. Seemed determined to not succumb to his charm.

Too fucking bad. He liked her, and by all that was unholy in his world, he'd make her feel the same about him. Even if he had to tie her to his damned bunk again and tongue lash her clit until she cried for mercy.

On second thought, that sounded pretty damned good.

Peering down at her, the crown of her red head not even reaching his chin, he almost tossed her over a shoulder and gave in to his deviously erotic plan.

But then she'd probably get all pissy because they'd

missed out on a chance to find her fucking brother. The things he did to get laid.

He kept his hand firmly on the bare skin of her back—a gentlemanly guide for a lady—and added in a proper, scowling glare that indicated she was not to be messed with.

She might be able to fight, but anything that attacked her here wouldn't do so with fair numbers or advantage. She had too much confidence in her ability.

He, on the other hand, was pragmatic.

As he left the pier and his boat, he had to trust the idiots to watch it. This small port in the Dominican wasn't the nicest place to visit. His boss, Henderson, didn't have dominion here. Or so Gavin was led to believe. Then again, the boss had many branches to his business he knew nothing about. Gavin usually didn't care. In his world, only his shit and welfare counted.

Knowing this place was a bit rougher than others, ruled by a gang who was both ruthless and double dealing, why would Steph's brother be here? And why visit a brothel? Other than the obvious.

But seriously, sex for hire thrived in the islands. One didn't have to visit this rough, drug trade fueled town to find it.

As they entered the wharf area, the noise level rose. Dozens of people barking, the hum of many motors, and even blaring radios filled the air. While not a long distance, their destination was farther than he wanted to take Steph by foot. He'd saved her sandals when he hid her clothes, but the longer they walked, the more likely someone would try something stupid.

And then he'd have to kill, which would then cause issues with his boss given someone was bound to deduce he worked for Henderson—because while his face might not be well known his boat was. Since he wasn't keen on a lecture or starting a war with another gang, best he avoid the issue altogether.

He caught the eye of a fellow with a utility style golf cart with the wave of his fingers.

When Gavin mentioned the place they wanted to go, the grizzled fellow gave them a knowing smile, his yellow teeth less offensive than his breath. Gavin requested the scenic route, less to see the scenery than to ensure they lost any tails that might want to see where they were going.

They hopped onto the back of the cart, the shelf space a perfect perch that gave him an excuse to wrap his arm around Steph to prevent her falling off.

She'd not said much since they left the boat. It worried him. She probably plotted his demise—or her escape.

The bouncy ride took them right into the heart of town, then past it, winding up the hillside, the din of the town receding behind them as the lushness of the jungle crowded close. He relaxed a bit as they left the town behind. Less likely they'd be attacked out here.

The steep hill put them at an incline. He wrapped one arm around the bar of the cart that went to the roof, the other stayed anchored around her waist.

To his surprise, she slid her arm around him, hugging him close. For a moment, he basked in the proximity before her true purpose was revealed.

Bracing his feet on the fender, he caught her wrist before she could fully pull the knife from the sheath at his hip. "What are you planning to do with my knife?"

"Shave my legs?" she said, blinking at him innocently.

"Put it back, Ariel."

"What if I don't want to?" The wrist he'd captured tugged, as if she could free herself. Adorable and so unlikely.

"Then don't, but don't cry about the consequences."

"What consequences?"

Since his arm around her allowed his hand to palm her stomach, it was quite simple to move it to her thigh. His fingers slid under the hem of her skirt.

"What are you doing?" she asked, the query somewhat breathy.

"Punishing you."

"By doing what?"

He cupped her mound, barely hidden by the scrap of fabric that was supposed to pass as panties. The heat of her scorched, and the crotch of her panties was damp already.

"You're wet, Ariel."

"It's hot."

"Is that all it is?" He rubbed her.

Her thighs pressed tight, but his hand was already trapped, and he kept stroking.

"Stop it."

"Put the knife back."

"You think you can tease me into doing it?" She laughed, a high-pitched sound. "Go ahead. I'm not giving it back."

"Good. I'd rather you disobey. I'm going to enjoy this." He already was. His cock was rock hard, his hand titillating.

"Then you'll enjoy it alone, because I certainly

won't." Such stubborn denial. She even braced herself, her whole body rigid, determined to fight.

As if she'd win.

He bent his head as he pressed the heel of his hand against her sex, and his lips found hers for a hungry kiss. How sweet she tasted to him. He took great pleasure in the fact her mouth immediately clung to his. In short order they were nibbling at each other's mouths, their tongues intertwined.

Her thighs relaxed and he managed to tug the damp crotch of her panties aside. His fingers brushed her sex, the pulsing heat almost scorching the tips.

The jostle of the cart as it hit a rough spot meant his hand cupped her, squeezed her so much that his fingers slid into her and she gasped.

The path evened out and he let his mouth trail the smooth column of her neck, downwards to the valley between the slashing bands of fabric. He wanted to brush his face across the sharp points of her nipples protruding from the fabric, but their position didn't lend itself to that kind of foreplay.

Instead, he brushed his fingers over her clit, slick with her juices, swollen and eager for his touch.

She whimpered. "Stop."

"What if I don't want to?" He rubbed her clit some more, feeling her body shiver against him.

A loud moan escaped her. "Stop."

"Put the knife back."

"No. You can't do this." She panted the words, her head leaning back, her eyes closed, her legs spread for him to touch her fully.

He fingered her, the tightness of her cunt a pleasure and a torture because he couldn't fuck her, not yet.

"Why can't I do this?" he teased as he thrust a second finger into her, drawing a sharp gasp.

"The driver..."

"Is probably enjoying what he's hearing." And more important. Gavin was staking his claim. "Don't worry," he said, whispering in her ear. "Only I can see and feel just how hot and wet that cunt of yours is. I'm tempted to hop off right now and push you up against a tree so I can fuck you."

"We—we—" She couldn't seem to finish that thought as his fingers plunged in and out, in and out.

"Just say the word, Ariel, and I'll have your skirt up around waist, and my cock buried balls deep in that cunt of yours."

"Yes. No. Oh God. Oh God."

Despite the temptation, he didn't jump from the cart. Instead, he stroked her. Finger fucked her tight channel, and dammit if her hips didn't try and roll with his thrusts, undulating against his hand. For the first time, she searched him out for a kiss, her lips mashing against his, her teeth nipping his lower lip.

He kept rubbing her, his thumb stroking her clit, his fingers buried deep in that heated channel. She panted against his mouth, mewled too.

Over and over, he thrust his fingers into her, his cock aching for relief and yet, he abstained. This was for her, and her alone.

Her sweet cunt squeezed his fingers, her whimpers faster. He watched her face and saw the moment her orgasm hit. Felt it too. But even more glorious, her eyes opened, their green depths glazed with passion, and from her lips just a single whispered word.

"Gavin."

He would have given her anything in that moment.

As the tremors of her climax subsided, he felt the knife return to his sheath, but he didn't care. She could keep the knife because she rested her head on his shoulder and sighed.

Not in exasperation, or weariness.

She sighed in pleasure and relaxed against him in trust.

In that moment, he came to a startling realization. *I love her.* And no matter what, he would never let her go.

― ― ― ― ―

CHAPTER NINETEEN

― ― ― ― ―

HOLY FUCK.

She'd just come, in public, on the back of a golf cart. Come hard.

Trembled still with aftershocks. But once the tremors in her body began to subside, her reasoning returned. Indignation followed, and she tried to grab the knife again, only Gavin caught her hand before she managed to even pull it from the hilt.

"I'm going to kill you!" she almost yelled, but conscious now of their audience—unlike a few minutes ago when she was riding his hand like a horse for the finish line—she curbed the level of her vehemence. "How dare you."

"I told you to put the knife back."

"You played dirty."

"Because I made you come? Shouldn't you be thanking me? After all, it was all about your pleasure. I got nothing out of it."

"Bullshit," she spat. "You totally got off on doing that."

"So what if I did? I warned you, but you refused to listen. One might say you left me no choice." He didn't appear in the least contrite. Actually, he appeared smug.

"It wasn't right."

"Neither was you trying to take my knife."

"Maybe if you'd given me something to defend myself with I wouldn't have to steal yours."

"You should trust me to protect you."

"Zola says to trust no one."

"In most cases, Zola is right. But not about me."

"And why should I suddenly trust you?"

"Because," he said as the cart pulled to a stop and he jumped off. "I'm going to help you find your brother."

She eyed him suspiciously. "I thought you didn't know my brother."

"I don't. But I do have connections."

"What kind of connections?" she asked, ignoring his hands to land on the ground by herself.

"The kind that will hopefully keep us safe in this den of inequity." Gavin moved away from her to hand their driver—a grinning driver who made her want to scrub herself—a few bills.

Yet it wasn't the knowing look from their ride that made her snap. It was the cocky grin on Gavin's face that made her lose control. She dove at him, nails extended.

Catching her by the wrist, Gavin easily halted her attack. He always did, to her shame. Zola would have mocked her for being so weak. Then again, Zola was to blame making Steph think all this time she was stronger than she was.

"Do I have to punish you again, Ariel? This time I guarantee we'll have an avid audience." He indicated the building at their back with its many windows. "But if you keep pushing me, I will bend you over and fuck you right here."

"You wouldn't dare."

"Try me." His eyes were half-shuttered, his words a low growl as he yanked her hard against him. "I'm more than willing, as you can feel." He ground himself against her.

"Is sex all you can think of?" she asked.

"When I'm around you? Yes."

There was a perverse compliment in there some- where and she warmed even as she prepared to retort.

Except there was a sudden commotion as the doors to the building opened. Men poured out. Armed men.

Gavin cursed. "Fuck me, someone must have warned them I was coming."

"What do they want?"

"Probably my fucking head. I'm a wanted man, remember. Run, Ariel," he said, turning to face the approaching men, knife in one hand, gun in the other. "Get to the boat. Gunner and Lash will get you out of here."

Run?

"Let me help you."

"I can handle this. But in case I don't, you don't want to be around. You know what they'll do to you."

She did. And he was right. Unarmed and at a size disadvantage, what kind of help could she give?

I can't just leave him.

Why did she care? This was her chance to escape. Let him deal with the thugs. They obviously had a problem with him.

She took off running, closing her ears to his shouted taunts, the cries of pain, the crack of gunfire. Only two shots. None of them hit her.

Yet she still hurt. The shame of her cowardice wounded, and yet, common sense told her she made the right choice.

Zola taught me to fight bare-handed.

She also taught Steph to know when the odds were stacked against her.

The thin sandals she wore weren't made for tearing through the jungle, but sliding down escarpments of dirt and making a straight line back to the harbor meant she hit the town streets quicker than expected, considering the golf cart's meandering path up the mountain.

The hard packed stone and dirt of the roads allowed her to easily run, her feet pounding past buildings, their facades bright and colorful, the curious faces in the windows and outside a blur.

One idiot along her route thought the jogging woman an easy target. She was too adrenalized to think twice about hitting him in the solar plexus and dropping him to the ground. The short knife in his hand made its way into her sweaty grip, and she continued to lope to the ship, wondering what kind of sight she made.

There were plenty of spots she could have stopped and asked for help. Called Zola—she knew her number by heart. She could have even contacted the compound. One of her adopted cousins or uncles would have come to her rescue. The options available to escape Gavin were numerous. She ignored them all as she made a beeline to his ship—because no matter their complicated relationship, she wasn't done with him yet.

She just hoped he lived because she was going back just as soon as she got better weapons, some clothes where her crotch wasn't hanging out, and reinforcements.

Stalking up the dock, snarling at a few sea dogs who dared look her way, she made it to the ship and found Lash on deck winding some rope.

"What are you doing here alone?" He eyed her and frowned. "And why does it look like you wrestled a forest?"

Her mad dash through the jungle left its mark. Great. She grimaced. "I need a gun."

"A gun for what?" Lash asked, just as Gunner swung out of the wheelhouse and barked, "Where's Gavin?"

"Some whorehouse in the hills." She pointed off in the distance. "Possibly dead. I don't know, but I was planning to go back and find out."

"I warned that moron to take us with him." Gunner shook his head.

"Since when does he need help?" scoffed Lash. "Something must have distracted him." A pair of gazes fixed on her with accusation.

"Don't blame me for this. I was just along for the ride. I don't think he was expecting a reception."

"He should have given who's running the place." Gunner and Lash exchanged a knowing look.

She couldn't help but ask. "Who?"

"She who must not be named."

Not liking the answer, she kicked Lash in the shin.

"Ow, not nice."

"Answer me then," she snapped. "Or next time, I'll aim higher."

"She's mean," Lash pouted.

"She is," Gunner agreed. "Probably why Gavin likes her so much. And in answer to your question, a woman named Sasha runs that brothel you visited. She and Gavin used to date."

A big snort escaped Lash. "Date? They almost got married. Except they didn't because she was a big ol' whore. Gavin was the only one who didn't seem to know that, so when he found out, he hated everyone for a while."

"He loved her?" For some reason, the idea of him caring for another woman tightened a vise around her heart.

"Used to. I'm pretty sure he's over it except for the part he's never had a steady girlfriend since," Gunner said.

"He says relationships are for suckers," Lash added.

"But I'm pretty sure he's changed his mind," Gunner quickly interjected. "I mean, look at the two of you."

"What about us?" she said. "He doesn't like me."

"What makes you think that?"

She rolled her eyes. "Because he's never said it."

"Yeah, but he doesn't need to. For one, he let you onto his boat," Gunner said.

"No he didn't. I hijacked it. He didn't have a choice."

"He chose to come after you," Lash pointed out.

"For revenge."

"He would have killed you if it was just revenge. He's pretty straightforward that way," Gunner said, and Lash nodded in agreement.

"If not for revenge, then why do you think he came

after me?" she asked. Could it be because he felt that same spark?

"Great sex," was Lash's prompt reply.

"It's more than that." Gunner shook his head. "He is an idiot, and so are you if you don't see the fact he cares about you."

He did? Or were they just feeding her wishful thinking? Either way, she knew what had to be done. "Whatever. I didn't come back to the boat to get in a debate about whether he likes me or not. Do you think he's alive?"

"Probably."

She almost sagged in relief. "Then who's coming with me to save his sorry ass?"

"Save the mighty Gavin and have him owe us? I'm in," Lash exclaimed.

"Me too, obviously. Guard the boat," Gunner said, walking past her.

She planted her hands on her hips. "Excuse me? I am not staying behind."

"You can't come with us," Gunner argued. "Gavin would totally skin us alive if anything happened to you."

"I can help."

"Yes, you can," Lash agreed. "By not getting us into trouble."

Her short stature didn't prevent her leap to grab hold of Lash's ear and yank down. He yelped and she growled. "Stop fucking around. Gavin needs us. So get me some weapons and some decent fucking clothes, and let's get moving. Or I'll gut you where you stand and let the gulls pick at your entrails."

"You and Gavin are so made for each other," Gunner snorted with a smile.

Oddly enough, she didn't take offense at his statement.

Maybe an orphan and a mercenary could have a happily ever after.

Or at least really good sex for a while.

CHAPTER TWENTY

A FEW MORE YANKS AND THREATS TO LASH'S EAR GOT her armed with a small handgun and a knife. But this only occurred after they tried to lock her in the wheel-house. It didn't happen and Gunner still shot her dirty looks as he cupped his groin.

His fault for thinking he could mansplain how dangerous rescuing Gavin would be.

She knew there would be danger, and it wasn't going to stop her for a few reasons. Not only was that brothel —and its whore of an owner—possibly keeping Gavin prisoner—or responsible for his death, which meant vengeance—but there might be a clue to her brother's disappearance somewhere inside.

Nothing could keep her away.

She tried to remain positive as they climbed on foot back to the property, not wanting to arrive publicly via golf cart like she had before. It took longer, though, which she wasn't happy about. By her calculations, she was at least ten, fifteen minutes racing back to the boat, then another five getting armed, and now at least twenty going back because her reinforcements wouldn't run.

"Only pussies run," Lash advised her. And bloody Gunner agreed.

So they walked. Quickly. She worried, while they remained fairly nonchalant. The idiots, who whacked their way through the foliage with machetes, seemed to think Gavin's ex-girlfriend wouldn't hurt him.

That reassured her a little because she didn't want Gavin harmed. She also didn't want him touched by any hands but her own. Would he be upset if she cut off his ex-girlfriend's hands?

The trek uphill to the brothel took longer than expected. Once they got close, they slowed and stopped to assess the situation, spying through the foliage. They faced an interesting dilemma. How to get in?

"We can't just walk through the front door. We'll be stopped right away," Gunner declared. "Place like this will have a guy, maybe two scanning customers."

She mused aloud. "Do you think there's a side entrance we can use to sneak in?"

"Probably, but it won't be any less guarded. This is an upscale place. The kind where they serve clients in real glass and not plastic cups," Gunner said.

"They even make the girls shower," Lash remarked.

Why wouldn't they shower? Shudder.

"There is one way you could probably get in," Gunner said, rubbing his chin. "Take off your shirt, fluff up your hair, and hit the front door to demand an audition."

"An audition to be a prostitute?" she said with a glare.

"Hey, you asked for ideas."

"Why don't you shake your thing and get us inside?" she retorted with a pointed arch of her brow. "Show us what you've got. Come on. Whip it out. Let's get a peek at the goods."

Gunner turned a shade of pink and stammered, "Men don't do that."

"I would!" Lash volunteered.

In the end, no one got naked, because it turned out the side entrance only had one guy guarding it. When he moved away from his post for a smoke, Lash took him out with a hard left hook.

The guard hit the dirt face first and they were in.

Upon entering the building, they found themselves in a laundry room with an industrial sized washer and a clothes rack strung with tiny unmentionables. When she noted Gunner pocketing a G-string, he shrugged and mouthed, "It's not for me."

Then who? Suddenly remembering the outfit she'd worn earlier that day, she felt an urge to shower.

Moving deeper in to the massive house, they kept away from the kitchen where they heard the sounds of pots and pans, running water, and a radio playing soft Latin music.

They crept quietly across the terra cotta floor, the quiet inside at odds with the strange rooms they passed through, one strewn with velvet and brocade covered divans. Another with a stage at one end, and a bar running down the side. Then there was the room with just a swing in the middle with a dildo projecting from the seat.

They encountered a few guards on their way, Gunner and Lash moving quickly and efficiently to stifle them before they could cry out.

But their luck wouldn't last. Someone would notice them at one point and raise an alarm. In the meantime, each guard they incapacitated, knocked out and tied up, usually with their own belt, was one less to face later on.

When she and Gavin had been attacked, she'd noted at least twelve men. By her count, they'd now taken care of five. Leaving seven, possibly more, out there. Easy peasy.

Wandering the main floor, clearing out two more guards as they did, she realized they'd have to go up a level to continue their search since they'd come up empty-handed. There was no hidden doorway to a basement or cellar.

Creeping up the stairs, her heart just about stopped when she heard the rumble of a male voice. His voice, but it appeared muffled.

Upon reaching the landing, she put a finger to her lips and had the two guys flank the plantation shutter-style doors closing off the room where she heard the voice. There was no way to investigate the inside without being seen, so she pressed her ear against the door to try and decipher the situation.

"Much as it's been nice catching up, I really should leave," Gavin said, his tone terse.

Having spent some time with him, Steph recognized his moods enough to know he sounded displeased. Had he suffered while she wasted time getting help and returning?

"Leave?" Laughter tinkled. Feminine laughter. "But it's been so long. We have so much to catch up on."

That must be the ex-girlfriend. Steph's lips pressed tight.

"I'm not in the mood for more chitchat. I have shit to do. And you have a business to run."

"Ah yes, my business. Sex sells." Again that annoying titter. "I've done well for myself. So have you. Rumor has it you've got a nice place by the ocean."

"It's adequate."

"I'd love to see it."

Not without eyes you won't, Steph thought with a snarl.

Gunner put a hand on her arm and shook his head, then mouthed, "Gonna check over there." He and Lash headed off down the hall to peek in the other rooms.

She kept listening.

"Would you can the platitudes and shit?" Gavin made a noise. "You seem to think we're friends, Sasha."

"Aren't we? We used to be more than friends once upon a time."

"Until you fucked your way through everyone I knew."

Oooh, way to let her have it.

"You're not still mad about that, are you? It was so long ago."

Ha! As if he'll fall for that.

"You're right. It was. Water under the bridge."
Hunh?

"I knew you couldn't stay mad at me forever. I've missed you ever so much. You and that lovely fat cock of yours. It's been so long since I had a taste."

Excuse me? Jealousy widened Steph's eyes and she suddenly didn't give a damn who was in the room. She kicked the slatted doors open and burst in, pistol in one hand, knife in the other.

Just in time, too, given the blonde falling out of a tiny bikini was kneeling in front of Gavin.

Oh, hell no. "Move away from him, bitch," Steph snarled, stepping into the room.

"Ariel! What are you doing here?"

"What's it look like I'm doing?" she snapped.

"Did you come to save me?" Gavin grinned at her, whereas she scowled.

"Where are the chains holding you down?" Because for a prisoner, he looked remarkably unfettered.

"Only you like tying me up." He winked.

"Who the fuck are you?" yelled the woman.

"Your worst nightmare." Yeah, she resorted to a cliché.

"Get out."

"Where's my brother?" Steph asked, pointing the gun.

"Guards!" Gavin's ex screamed, and Steph dove for her, only to have the blonde dance out of reach.

"Tell me where my brother is," Steph demanded again, pacing the woman.

"Don't tell me your brother is the only reason you came back," huffed Gavin.

She shot him a glare. "Did you really think I came for you? And don't act all pissy. You obviously weren't in any danger, other than having your knob polished."

"She never laid a hand on me."

"Only because I interrupted," she snapped.

"I'll have you know I had no intention of fucking her."

"Sure you didn't."

"I was going to find out about your brother, but then you interrupted."

"You mean you were using me?" Sasha screeched. "You fucking bastard."

"You didn't really think I'd forgiven you?" Gavin's steely gaze perused Sasha and he smirked. "I've moved on to much better things."

"If you say that hag over there—"

"Watch who you're calling a hag you old slut," Steph held the gun steady. One bullet would shut her up.

"I am not old!"

"Whatever you tell yourself when you lather on the lotion at night, honey." Steph smirked as the other woman turned red.

More might have been said, but a few guards chose that moment to run in. With a sigh of annoyance, Steph tossed the pistol at Gavin.

"You take care of them while I handle her," she said. She hefted the knife from hand to hand, noting how Sasha's eyes followed the motion.

"You'll pay for this," the blonde spat.

"You're not in a position to make threats," Steph remarked, advancing on her. "Where's my brother? Where's Ronin?"

"Ronin?" No mistaking the lilt that indicated she recognized the name.

"Yes, Ronin. Big tattooed guy."

"I know who you mean. He's that pain in the ass who showed up here, out of the blue, and tried to take one of my girls."

"Where did he go?"

"How would I know? Crusty Seadog, my boss, got involved and took care of it." Sasha tossed her hair and looked smug.

At the name, Steph whirled and fixed Gavin with a glare. He'd tucked the gun in the back of his pants and used his fists to lay a guy flat.

She stalked over to him, waving her knife. "You liar! You said you didn't know about my brother."

"I don't."

"Bullshit. She says you took him." Steph jabbed the knife in Sasha's direction.

The bitch laughed. "You think Gavin is Crusty Seadog?"

Confused, Steph glanced from Sasha to Gavin. "What's going on? Isn't that your name?"

"Nope."

"Impossible. I heard it. During the fight. And even before that."

Gavin inclined his head. "Blame Gunner and Lash. Their idea of a joke."

"You mean you aren't the guy I was looking for?" Her eyes widened. "Oh, shit. I kidnapped the wrong dude."

"You did."

"Fuck. Fuck. Fuck." The depths of her stupidity bitch-slapped her. She stalked back to Sasha who backed away, hands held in front of her.

Steph snarled, "Where's your boss?"

"I don't know."

Steph leaned in close with her knife. "You'd better figure it out quick, or I'm going to carve him a bloody message in your skin."

"I swear. I don't know." Steph pressed the tip of the knife and the woman hiccupped in fear. "But if I had to guess, I'd try his estate. It's somewhere on the far side of the island."

"Was that so hard?" Steph asked.

"Go ahead and find him," Sasha spat. "You'll die. You and your little army of boy toys are no match for his men. Your brother thought he could challenge Crusty Seadog, and failed."

Ronin fail? She wouldn't believe it. "We'll see about that," Steph said a little too sweetly. "And by the way, *honey*, next time you put your hands on my man, I will do more than stab you." To make her point, she jabbed the blade into Sasha's skin, deep enough to puncture the silicone based tit.

Steph whirled away as Sasha screeched and wailed. "I'm leaking. You bitch. Do you know how much these cost?"

Steph met Gavin's gaze and he cocked a brow. "Was that necessary?"

From where Steph was standing? "Totally." Then she strutted past him. Angry at him. Angry at herself.

Out in the hall, she came face to face with a guard who hurriedly pointed a gun at her.

With a bellow that sounded oddly enough like Gavin shouting, "Don't you fucking touch her," Gavin went charging past, body slamming the fellow before he could get off a shot.

They grappled on the floor, and it occurred to Steph she could help Gavin. Instead, she stepped over their bodies and skipped down the stairs.

He can save himself. She'd obviously made a mistake.

Stupid lying jerk.

She'd almost made it out the front door when Gavin caught up and spun her around. "Where do you think you're going?"

"To save my brother."

"You heard Sasha. He's probably in Seadog's compound."

"And?"

"What do you mean 'and?' You can't just march in there and demand him back. It's suicide."

"I don't care. He's my brother."

"I'm pretty sure your brother wouldn't want you to kill yourself finding him."

"Who cares what you think? You're a liar." She pulled at his grip, then screamed and kicked when she couldn't break free.

"Why are you so pissed?" he asked, reeling her close, trapping her body.

"I don't know what you're talking about. I am not mad," she muttered.

"Is this about the whole Crusty thing?"

"No." Yes. She was angry at herself over the mistake. She should have made sure he was the right man instead of wasting her time. Yet, the real simmer came from jealousy and having her eyes opened to the kind of woman Gavin really liked. Voluptuous, tall, blonde with big tits. In other words, the exact opposite of Steph.

How did I ever think I stood a chance of being with him?

"It's not a big deal. So what if you mistook me for someone else."

She pounded at him. "It was a big deal because that someone was who I needed to ask about my brother. All this time I've wasted. Because you lied."

His lips pursed. "I'm sorry. I guess I didn't think of that."

"No you didn't," she said, wrenching free from him. She stormed towards the door only to have Gavin plant himself in her path.

"I'm ready and willing to help you now."

Anger wouldn't let her accept the offer. "Move," she ordered.

"Not until you listen to me."

"Listen to what? More lies?"

Their gazes were locked, which was probably why he never caught her knee coming up. While she delivered a good, solid blow, he didn't cry like a pussy, nor did he crumple.

A dangerous glint entered his eyes. "That was not cool."

"Neither was what you did, so I guess that makes us even."

"What you did was way worse. You should offer to kiss it better."

She snorted. "Like hell. Why don't you get Sasha to do it? She was getting pretty cozy with you when I walked in."

His brow creased, but soon smoothed as he smiled. "Holy shit, you're jealous."

"Am not," she retorted. "Why the hell would I care who you fuck? Now get out of my way. I gotta go find my brother."

Her words wiped the smile from his face. "You can't go there. I forbid it."

"You what?" She gaped at him for a second before laughing hysterically. "Fuck off." She feinted to the left, and when he followed, darted past him, squeezing through the gap and running.

She exited onto the front lawn past Gunner who was seated in a golf cart, past Lash who pulled a body out of the way, and into the jungle.

In what was becoming a familiar place, she ran and slid through the trees. The only sound she heard was that of her panting breath—and the crushing disappointment as she noted a lack of pursuit.

Good riddance. She didn't need Gavin. Didn't need his high-handed attitude. Or his chauvinistic nature. Or his lies.

I should have known he was too hot for a shitty name like Crusty Seadog.

Pausing for a moment to catch her breath, she could only let out a squeak as she suddenly found herself lifted off the ground and thrown over a muscular shoulder.

"Put me down!" she yelled.

"Nope." Gavin began climbing back the way they'd come, effortlessly, the jerk.

"I don't want to go anywhere with you."

"Too bad."

"I hate you," she yelled, pounding on his back.

"Stop that."

"No." She laced her hands together and swung at him, her locked fists hitting him in the lower back.

He retaliated by smacking her ass.

Hard.

Shock rounded her mouth. "You did not just do that!"

"Keep acting like a child and I will do it again."

"Fuck you!" She hit him.

He slapped her butt in the same, throbbing spot. "Behave," he barked.

"No."

Her reply earned her another spank.

"Stop it," she shrieked.

"You stop it first."

She bit him.

He bit her back on the leg.

"I hate you."

"Says the woman who infiltrated a brothel to save me."

"I didn't care what happened to you," she lied. "I was looking for my brother."

"And me." Said so smugly.

"No, I wasn't. Sasha can have you."

"I can hear that jealousy talking again."

She pummeled him and, in reply, he tightened his grip over her legs with one arm, but his free hand slid between her thighs. She was wearing shorts again, a pair filched from his drawers and cinched tight. Long, loose, and baggy, yet that didn't prevent her from feeling the tips of his fingers rubbing at her sex.

And enjoying it.

A whistle sounded. "That's it. Show her who's boss."

"Shut it or I will rip out your tongue," Gavin growled.

"Is that any way to thank us after we came your rescue?" Lash said, managing to sound aggrieved.

"Yeah," Gunner agreed. "We risked life and limb to free you from the manicured claws of your ex-girlfriend."

"You're lucky I am letting you live given you brought Steph into danger. What the fuck were you thinking?" Gavin railed.

"Don't blame us. Blame her. She wouldn't take no for an answer. Insisted we had to go save you." Gunner exclaimed. "She's bossy."

"And mean," Lash added.

Steph wanted to die of mortification. "Am not," she mumbled.

A snort escaped Gavin. The hand between her

thighs nudged her and she wanted to moan. Then curse because how could she be getting aroused?

It wasn't fair.

"I found us some wheels," Gunner noted.

"If you wanna drive, I'll hold on to your woman," Lash offered.

No mistaking the meaty sound of a fist hitting flesh.

Gavin spoke. "Gunner, you drive. Lash, you take the passenger seat and watch for anyone following. I'll hold Steph in the back."

And he meant that quite literally. He seated himself on the bench, and settled her on his lap.

She might have protested more, but dammit, it felt good to be in his arms. Especially since it wouldn't happen for much longer.

She knew where to look for Ronin, and once she found him, back to the compound she would go. Ronin would insist, and she'd quite frankly had enough adventure for a while. Gavin would sail off in search of new conquests and it would be as if this exciting interlude never happened.

Maybe Gavin will ask me to stay.

You heard what his friends said. He doesn't do relationships.

Foolish her, she kind of wished he did.

CHAPTER TWENTY-ONE

Having Steph on his lap was a form of unexpected torture.

Gavin had been so worried about her when Sasha's guards had attacked him. Wondered if she'd gotten away safely. If he'd ever see her again.

He'd gotten knocked out by sheer numbers only to regain consciousness, the guest of a woman he still hated.

A woman he found repulsive with all the artifice. Nothing like his Ariel with her natural beauty and reddish locks.

When Steph appeared suddenly, a vengeful fiery goddess intent on rescue, his first impulse was to grab her and kiss her.

Then she tried to run from him.

Didn't she yet grasp he would never let her go? How many times did he have to imprint himself on her body for her to understand they belonged together?

Tell her. Tell her how you feel.

He wanted to. Knew he should. But couldn't. The words just wouldn't emerge.

Real men don't talk about their feelings.

He remembered his dad saying that. He also remembered his dad dying alone, an ornery fucking bastard who drove everyone away.

As soon as Gavin hit the deck of his boat, he barked orders. "Get us out of here. Full speed once you hit the open sea. Watch for signs of pursuit."

"No," Steph exclaimed. "We can't leave. You heard what she said. My brother is on this island."

"And so are the enemies we've just made. We can't stick around. They'll just converge en masse and pick us off."

"But—"

"We'll come back, Ariel. We just need a plan that doesn't get us killed. Trust me."

For a second, he truly expected her to protest some more. She was good at arguing, yet she went silent, and with his friends at the helm, he took her below deck, a sense of urgency imbuing him.

She waited until he'd set her down before turning on him and pummeling his chest. "I'm tired of you manhandling me and not giving me a say."

He grabbed her wrists and yanked her against him. "I wouldn't have to manhandle you if I thought you would behave and not run off to do stupid things."

"You mean stupid things like saving your ass? Don't worry, I regret not escaping when I had the chance."

"Why not just admit you can't stand the thought of leaving me?" He wanted her to say it. Never mind he wouldn't, perhaps if he heard the words slip from her lips, he'd find the will to say what was in his heart.

"You think awfully highly of yourself," she said.

"You're right. I do. And I think you do, too."

"Do not."

"Must you always argue?" he said. He towered over her, his hands still firmly gripping her wrists down at her sides, not allowing any space between their bodies. She peeked up at him, not at all intimidated by him. No fear in her expression. Nothing but heat. A heat he recognized.

Her cheeks flushed and her gaze dropped to his mouth.

He'd waited long enough. He dipped his head to claim her lips, the fierceness of his need matched by her own.

The taste of her only served to fire his boiling blood. He released her hands that he might touch her, let his palms skim over her frame, reassuring himself she remained uninjured. That she was here. With him. And never leaving.

She clutched at his shoulders, fingers digging into his flesh, drawing him closer. Deny it all she might, there was no pretense she could hide behind once they touched.

With deft fingers, he divested her of her clothes, baring her to his touch, her soft skin rubbing against him. She tugged at his shirt, and in her haste, buttons popped. Not that he cared. The urgency of her desire only fueled his own arousal.

She grappled with his pants, and he had to help her, the leather snug, but once unzipped, his cock sprang forward, ready and willing.

The bed lay only paces away, too far. He cupped her ass, those full sweet cheeks, and hoisted her.

Despite this being a new position for them both, she instinctively wrapped her legs around his waist, pressing her wet cunt against his lower belly.

Adjusting her meant he could tuck his cock between their bodies and with a little bounce, rub it against her slick cleft.

That earned him a glorious moan.

He grunted as he kept rubbing and couldn't help but mutter a husky, "Tell me you want me."

"Please, Gavin."

The soft plea was enough for him.

He shifted their bodies yet again, aiming the tip of his cock at that slick opening. Her head went back as he slid into her, wedging his cock into that tight cunt, feeling the glorious heat of her body clenching all around him.

"Fuck that feels good," he whispered before finding her lips. He thrust into her, his hands holding her steady for his in and out pumps.

He leaned her against a wall, and devoted himself to driving his cock deep, aiming for that sweet spot, the one that when hit caused her to clench and cry out.

"That's it, come for me," he murmured. "Come all over my cock."

"Yes. Yes." The words were panted moans. Her fingers dug into his shoulders.

He thrust faster. Harder. In and out, until her cunt rippled around him. The tremor of her orgasm fisted him tight, and only when she uttered a long, drawn-out moan did he let himself spill inside her.

Spill with nothing between them.

Slowly, the passion subsided. Their bodies cooled and yet he didn't want to set her down. Didn't want to separate the intimate joining of their bodies. Didn't want to fight.

"Truce?" he asked.

Cheeks still flushed, her heavy-lidded green gaze settled on him. "What would the terms entail?"

"If you promise not to escape, to stay with me without attempting to tie me up, or toss me overboard, then I will help you find your brother."

"Really?" She frowned. "Why?"

He shrugged. "Maybe because I feel like doing something altruistic for once."

Her brow arched.

He laughed. "Okay, maybe because while you were sleeping, I found out some shit about this Crusty Seadog character that I am not crazy about."

"Do you think he's killed Ronin?"

He hated the worried look in her eyes. But he wouldn't lie to her. Not on this. "Maybe. Unless he's got a use for him. In which case, he probably just locked him up."

"How do we find out for sure?" she asked.

"We'll have to find a way to get some eyes and ears inside his compound."

"You mean bribe his staff. That will take too long."

"I agree. There are other ways."

"What ways?" she asked suspiciously.

"Let's just say I have friends in interesting places," Gavin replied.

To which she laughed.

He frowned. "What's so funny?"

"The idea of you and friends."

"Meaning?"

"Because you're so grumpy most of the time."

"No, I'm not."

She traced his features with the tip of her finger. "You look grumpy right now."

"Only because you're arguing with me."

"Are you going to spank me again?" Her eyes twinkled with mischief.

"I might."

"Wouldn't that break the terms of our truce?"

"We said no killing or tossing overboard, nothing about spanks."

Her lips twitched. "True. Perhaps I should have gotten more details. Such as, where do I sleep?"

"The bunk with me, but I doubt you'll get to do much of that." He couldn't help a leer.

"We need to find a way to let Zola know I'm fine."

"She already does."

When she opened her mouth to harangue, he pressed a finger against it. "Before you get all pissy, and as part of this new truce thing, I guess I should mention that your guardian has been in contact with me since last night when she got hold of my satellite phone number. She's very fond of texting."

"Why that sly bitch!" she huffed. "She's contacting the enemy instead of her dawta."

"About the enemy part. Would it help if I mentioned at this point that I work for Henderson?"

Her gaze narrowed. "You know Henderson?"

He nodded.

"That's who runs the compound I was raised in."

"So I heard from your foster mother."

"Exactly what else have you heard?"

He rolled his shoulders. "Not much. Other than you

were a hellion to raise, have a tendency to steal peach pie, are scared of frogs, and suck at cooking."

"Holy shit, did Zola leave me any secrets?"

"No. She replied to everything I asked."

She stared at him. "What do you mean asked?"

Now's your chance. Tell her how you feel.

He chickened out. "I wanted to know what I was dealing with, especially once I told Henderson I'd help find Ronin."

She slapped his chest.

"What was that for?"

"For making me think you were an asshole."

"I am an asshole."

A glare in his direction made him chuckle.

"Don't think I'm doing this out of the kindness of my heart. Henderson is offering me a nice bonus if I find him alive."

"So, you're doing this for money?" Her lips turned down.

Tell her you'd do it for free, for her.

"It's what mercenaries do."

"Of course it is." She turned away, shoulders slumped. "I guess the next step is to find my brother. Then once I do, I can leave."

No, you can't. But his lips still refused to say the words trapped inside.

But staying silent didn't mean he intended to let her go.

You might not realize it yet, Ariel, but we're going to be together a long time. He just had to convince her of it.

CHAPTER TWENTY-TWO

AFTER THE ODD CONVERSATION AND FIGHT AT THE
brothel, things with Gavin felt different.

And not just because he'd agreed to find Ronin for
her, or the fact it turned out they were on the same side.

They didn't quite stop fighting, they were both too
stubborn and hot headed for that, yet the verbal sparring had its own charm. But driving each other wild
wasn't all they did.

They talked. Strategized. Made love.

Yes, love. For her at least, there was no mistaking
what she felt for him.

It was, unfortunately, one-sided. He'd made it clear
he was only helping her for money.

As for his attraction to her, simple lust. Nothing
more than two people sexually compatible. He'd yet to
say anything to make her think it would go beyond their
mission to save her brother.

Speaking of that mission, through his contacts,
Gavin discovered exactly where this Crusty fellow had

his hideaway. Sasha had simply told them it was located on the far side of the island.

The reality was this compound rested atop a sheer cliff face, the mountainous crag accessible via a single road that wound through the jungle from the nearest town, via a well-protected bay, or by helicopter.

None of those entries were an option. Not if they wanted to live.

After two days of sailing, looking for a spot to land and make their way by foot, she knew Gavin was ready to give up. But Steph couldn't.

He scrubbed his hand through his hair and frowned. "The place is impenetrable. Short of an airstrike, we can't get in."

Steph took his suggestion literally. "We can't drop a bomb on it."

His expression eloquently said that she stated the obvious. "I know we can't. What I wish we did know was if your brother is there for sure. We could be wasting our time."

"You think he's dead, don't you?" Despite her heart insisting it couldn't be, her logical mind knew the truth.

He shrugged. "We can't know that for sure."

"But?" she prodded.

"It's been almost two weeks with no word. No demand for ransom. Nothing. You might have to face facts."

She turned from him, arms wrapped around her body. "You want me to give up."

"I want you to face reality."

"He's not dead."

"He might as well be." Gavin pointed to the craggy outcropping in the distance. "We can't get up there. And if we keep sailing around in circles, someone is going to come after us. As it is, I'm surprised no one has."

"Maybe we could contact him."

"It's been tried," he said flatly.

"You did? Why didn't you tell me?"

"Because there was nothing to tell. His people claim they have no idea who and what we're talking about."

"They're lying. You just want to quit because you don't know what it's like to care about someone. You're mister cool and untouchable. But when you love someone, you have to take risks. To—"

"Listen Ariel. There's something I should say—"

His phone rang, the shrillness of it interrupting their conversation.

Gavin sighed as he pulled it from his pocket and checked the screen. No surprise, it was Zola. Again. Her foster mother had a tendency to call at least three times a day, sometimes more, to check on Steph.

She rolled her eyes. "Not again. I swear, for a woman who shoved me out of the nest, and had me kidnapped by a mercenary, she's awfully clingy."

Gavin smiled. "At least she cares." He handed over the phone.

Steph answered. "What now?"

"Stephy?"

At the familiar male voice, she burst into tears, and Gavin lunged to rip the phone out of her hands.

"Who is this?" he barked.

Sobbing tears of joy, Steph managed a blubbery, "It's Ronin." She held out her hands. "Let me talk to him." Gavin handed back the phone and she managed to say, "Ronin," before her brother cut her off.

"Who the fuck was that? Where are you? Zola says

you're with some of Henderson's guys looking for me. Who is it? Did he touch you? Do I need to kill him?"

"I'm fine," she managed when Ronin ran out of breath. "I'm with Gavin."

"That womanizer!"

"You know him?"

"I know of him," her brother growled.

"Where are you? Where have you been?" she asked, relief giving way to curiosity.

"In the jungle. I got myself in a spot of trouble and it took me a bit of time to get out of it. I would have called, but lost my phone. Don't change the subject. What the fuck were you thinking, leaving the compound?"

"I was looking for you."

"You should have stayed put. You're too fragile to be out there in the world."

"I'm tougher than I look," she retorted. When Gavin smirked, she gut punched him.

That only made him laugh.

"You need to get your ass back home right this instant. On second thought, I'm coming to get you. Zola says the port we're in isn't far from your location."

"You don't have to come get me."

"It isn't a request. I'll be there in a few hours."

Click.

The phone went dead and she stared at it for a moment, unable to look at Gavin. Unable to handle it if he looked relieved that she'd finally be out of his life.

"That was my brother."

"So I gathered. He's all right."

She shrugged. "I guess. He didn't say much other than I shouldn't have left the compound. He thinks I can't take care of myself." The ire had her lifting her gaze.

Gavin looked less than pleased. "He's right. For all your fighting skills, you're a babe in the jungle. You need to be protected."

"I'd say it's too late to keep me away from the wild animals." Her pointed stare brought a ghost of a smile to his lips.

"So, what's the plan now, Ariel? Your brother is safe. Where we sailing too?"

"Nowhere." She tossed the phone at Gavin. "Ronin says he and Zola are coming to get me. I'm going home."

"Today?"

"In a few hours. You're getting your bunk back."

"I—" Whatever he might have said was interrupted by a yell from Gunner.

"Hey, cap'n. I've got some coordinates from Zola. We changing our course?"

For a moment, he hesitated and her heart fluttered. *Ask me to stay. Tell him to sail way. Kidnap me.*

Instead, he sighed and shouted back, "Set up a rendezvous. Looks like Ariel is going home."

Their time together had come to an end.

CHAPTER TWENTY-THREE

SHE LEFT.

The shock of it still left him frozen. She'd not even once looked back.

And I didn't say a damned thing.

Now he was numb, which was probably for the best because as soon as he began to thaw, the pain started.

A pain worse than anything he'd ever felt.

Unlike his breakup with Sasha, he wasn't angry. Not with Steph or anyone else.

Actually, that wasn't true. He was angry.

With himself.

Why didn't I say something? Why did he keep silent instead of telling her what was in his heart?

Because real men don't emasculate themselves for a woman.

Men also weren't supposed to cry and yet his eyes burned.

Must be something in the air.

When a man hurt, there was only one thing to do.

Get drunk.

That same night after she left—left and never looked

back—Gavin went on a drinking binge. After his third bar fight—and banishment to a dirty alley where he had to fight—he found himself realizing he needed somewhere safer to drink or he'd wake up with a knife in his gut.

The thought of sailing away on his boat or even going to his not oft seen home didn't appeal. He didn't want to be alone, feared what would happen if he had only his thoughts to occupy him, so he went to harass the only person he could think of.

His buddy Cole took one look at him when he arrived on the doorstep stinking of booze and snorted. "What the fuck happened to you?"

"A woman."

"What happened to never letting a chick get close you again?"

"I wasn't planning to. But I guess you and your woman were contagious." Gavin shot him a glare. "I blame you." He took a swing at his happy and healthy looking friend, hating Cole for opening his mind to the possibility of happiness only have his heart shattered.

Cole ducked his fist easily and grabbed it, yanking him inside. "Don't blame me because you fucked up."

"What makes you think I fucked up?"

"Because you're here bitching and moaning."

"I had nowhere else to go."

"What happened? Did she get tired of your ugly mug?"

"No. She seemed to like me well enough."

"Did you cheat on her?" Cole asked.

"Never!"

"Did she cheat on you?"

Gavin glared.

"Valid question considering what happened with Sasha," Cole pointed out.

"Honestly, I don't know why she left. We were getting along so good. In and out of bed. I don't know what happened," Gavin said, his tone morose.

"Did you fight?"

"We were always fighting. It was part of her charm." Gavin sighed. "I fucked up."

"How?"

"I might have given her the impression I wasn't into a relationship."

"So, you liked this chick but never said, hey, let's hook up a little more permanently?"

Gavin shook his head.

"Seeing as how you want this girl, why not give her a ring and tell her?"

And therein lay the dilemma. "What if she doesn't feel the same? Maybe she left because she wanted to."

Cole stared at him. "Are you really going to be a pussy about this?"

"What are you talking about?"

"I mean, you're being a fucking wuss. Tell her how you feel."

"Real men don't—"

Cole interrupted. "Don't feed me that line of bullshit your old man used to spout. We are not cavemen. It's called expressing your fucking feelings. You should try it sometime, especially if you like this woman. She's not a mind reader and she'd probably like it."

"Like what?" Lillie asked, waddling into the room. Her rounded belly projected in front of her and caught Gavin's gaze.

He'd known of the pregnancy, mocked Cole about

it, but now he looked at it with a new light. A new appreciation.

That's Cole's child in there. His legacy. His family.

Cole settled a warm gaze on his woman and she fired one back. The love between them palpable.

A longing stabbed Gavin. *I want what they have.*

Cole jerked a thumb at Gavin. "Dumbass here found a chick he liked, but instead of telling her he was hot for her, he let her walk."

"Seriously?" Lillie's gaze rounded on Gavin. She shook her head. "Men. I swear you're all stupid. Come here," she ordered imperiously, hands on her hips.

Rather than argue with a pregnant woman, Gavin approached only to gasp when she sucker punched him in the gut.

"What the fuck?"

"You deserve that for being a moron. Women need more than a good screw to stick around. Sometimes you need to use words, like 'I love you.' Or at least, 'Hey, I think you're pretty cool, wanna shack up for a while?'"

"What if she said no? What if—"

"She didn't feel the same way?" Cole smiled. "Like I said before, you're being a pussy. Yank your balls out of hiding and tell this chick how you feel."

"It's too late. She's gone back home."

"And? Are you going to give up that easily?" Lillie asked. "Cole invaded an armed compound to find me." She said it with pride.

"I did, and it was the smartest thing I ever did." Cole grinned as he wrapped his arms around Lillie and nuzzled her neck.

"I remember that raid." He should since Gavin was part of it. "You were allowed to kill people in your way.

Where's she's gone, I can't because she's surrounded by family."

"So you kidnap her without anyone the wiser," Lillie suggested.

"Surely you can abduct one woman?" Cole added. "Or are you finally admitting I'm the better smuggler? If you need help, just ask."

"Fuck you. I don't need your stinking help. I'll get her myself." The moment the words left his lips, and the idea took shape, something inside him eased and Gavin laughed.

Time to become the pirate he harbored inside. *I'm coming for you, Ariel.* This time, he wouldn't let pride get in the way of telling her what he felt, and if she wouldn't listen, then he knew how to torture her into admitting what she needed. *Me.*

CHAPTER TWENTY-FOUR

THE TRAINING YARD DIRT TASTED JUST AS STEPH recalled—dirty with a hint of despair.

As to why Zola knocked her down for the umpteenth time? Steph was depressed.

Full blown, didn't give a damn about the world, depressed.

The fact Ronin was home safe and sound with a hundred bug bites to prove his story didn't raise more than a minor smile. Apparently, he wasn't the one truly in danger.

I was. She'd gotten her heart stolen by a mercenary, and without it, she found it hard to give a damn about anything anymore.

"Dawta, why are you so slow?" scolded Zola.

"Maybe I'm coming down with a bug."

"Ain't never seen no bug that dragged your lip to the ground and made you sigh like the world was ending."

In a sense ,it had. Steph had found a man who lit up her world with the brilliance of his presence. Without him, it was—

"Ow!"

The sharp rap of her teacher's training baton across her knuckles had her glaring.

"Stop moping about that man," Zola ordered.

"I am not moping."

"I should hope not since you're the one who turned tail and ran."

"I did not run. I walked off his ship." And he did nothing to stop her.

"Why didn't you stay, since you obviously miss him?"

"I don't miss him."

Whack.

Steph glared as she sucked her knuckles. "Okay, so I miss him. What would you have me do?"

"For one thing, you shouldn't have left him."

"I couldn't exactly stay. We both knew once I found my brother I'd go home."

"And?"

"What do you mean and?" She threw up her hands. "He didn't ask me to stay. That's what."

"Did you ask?"

"What do you mean did I ask? Of course I didn't ask. I'm not pathetic." Steph wasn't about to beg.

"No, you're too proud. Which is almost the same thing."

She opened her mouth to deny it only to shut it. Had she let pride get in her way?

"The man likes you. A lot."

Steph's lips twisted. "The man liked fucking. I don't think the who really mattered?"

"Are you that dense?"

This time Steph avoided the whack of the stick and

she circled the training ground, matching Zola's steady pace.

"I'm not dense. He never said he wanted me."

"Because he showed it. Idiot. I raised an idiot." Zola shook her hands at the sky.

"Maybe you did. Thanks a lot for pointing out the fact I fucked up. You think I don't know that? You think it makes me happy?" Then to her horror, she burst into tears.

Tossing her practice stick to the ground, Steph stalked off, looking for a private place to shed yet more tears. Enough now to make her own salty lake.

What if Zola is right? What if he wanted me to stay and didn't know how to ask?

Too late now.

"Where are you going, dawta? We're not done."

"I—I—" More words would have to wait because the contents of her stomach heaved. Again.

She'd had a hard time keeping food down the last few days. Something was ailing her.

When she finished throwing up, Zola was there with a cloth for her to wipe her face.

"You gonna let him know about the child?"

"What?" Steph turned her head too fast and almost gave herself whiplash.

"The child. In your belly." When Steph blinked at her stupidly, Zola sighed. "Do I have to explain where babies come from again?"

Considering the first time involved dolls and profane language and drawings in the dirt that could never be erased from her mind, she shook her head. "I can't be pregnant."

"Because you practiced safe sex." The sarcasm was thick.

Steph bit her lower lip. "We only had sex a few times." Times a few more. "Oh, God." She buried her face in her hands. "What am I gonna do?"

"For starters, you should tell him."

"He'll think I'm trying to trap him. And I don't want that." Steph sighed. "I royally fucked this up."

"It's only too late if you give up. I didn't realize I'd raised my dawta to be a coward." Zola snorted. "If you want him, go after him."

"Ronin will never allow it."

"This isn't Ronin's decision. It's yours. You get to decide what to do with your life. Do you love this man?"

"Yes." The word came without hesitation.

"Then, what are you going to about it?"

Steph straightened. "Find him. See if he cares for me. And if he doesn't, tie him to a bed until he does."

"That's more like it." Zola clapped her on the back.

"But first," Steph said, facing the bucket. "I need to throw up again." Because the thought of putting her heart out there for him to possibly destroy made her even more nauseous than before.

However, the idea was planted. She would boldly go after the man she loved, and she told her brother so in no uncertain terms.

The asshole locked Steph in her room, supposedly for her own good. She'd have to remember to use that exact set of words when she castrated him.

Since she couldn't do anything until someone let her out, she went to sleep, only to startle awake at the feel of a hand over her mouth.

Instantly panicked, she thrashed until a low voice said, "If you don't stop, Ariel, I'll have to use the rope."

Gavin had come for her.

Oh my God. She almost burst into tears.

"I'm going to take my hand away. Try not to scream. I had a bitch of time getting in unnoticed."

Zola would be pissed he'd managed. The compound was supposed to be a secure place. Yet Gavin had braved it to come find her.

Why?

Her heart pounded with hope.

His fingers moved from her mouth and stroked her cheek.

"Why are you here?" she whispered. "My brother will kill you if he finds out."

"Then I guess we better make sure he doesn't." His teeth gleamed in the gloom as he smiled. "As to why, I couldn't stay away. I missed you, Ariel."

"You did?" Her heart just about stopped at hearing the admission.

"I fucked up, Ariel. I let you walk away, instead of telling you how I feel. And only once you were gone did I realize, I need you."

He needs me.

Surely this wasn't real. She must still be sleeping.

"Pinch me," she demanded.

"Why?"

"Because I don't want this to be a dream."

"Does this feel like a dream?" His lips claimed hers in a fiery kiss that ignited her body.

The embrace went on for a while, the wild passion that always rose between them consuming them, demanding to be fed. She couldn't help but run her hands over his body, reacquainting herself with the breadth of his shoulders, the taut muscles of his arms, the masculine scent of him.

He drew her onto his lap, the firmness of his erection poking at her backside, fueling her hunger.

When he drew away, she made a sound of protest and wrapped her arms around his neck, pulling him close.

His next words whispered over her lips. "Sail away with me, Steph. My boat's in the harbor stocked to go anywhere you want. Or if you'd prefer firm land, I have a place. If you don't like it, I'll buy another. I'll give you anything you want if you'll come with me."

"For how long?" she asked.

"Forever, if you'll have me." His voice had a husky quaver to it when he said, "I love you."

As if punched in the gut, air whooshed from her. "I don't care where we go so long as I'm with you. I love you so much. I'm sorry I left. I've been miserable without you."

"Good."

She leaned back to glare. "I tell you I'm unhappy and that's what you have to say?"

"Yeah, because that's exactly how I felt. Incomplete. Adrift. Alone. I don't know how it happened, Ariel, but you complete something in me. Something I didn't even know was missing until we met."

Her hand cupped his cheek. "I know what you mean. And just so you know, I was going to come find you. I'd made up my mind to go and told my brother."

"Is that why your door was locked from the outside?"

She nodded. "I couldn't stand to be another moment without you."

"Ariel." He growled her name as he kissed her again, his hands stripping the short night dress she wore, baring her skin to the scorching caresses of his mouth.

The heat of his touch had Steph arching, presenting her breasts to his mouth. He latched on to her nipple, sucking hard while his hand gripped the other, kneading the flesh.

She weaved her fingers into his silky hair, clutching at him as he tortured her. He sucked on her nipple, lavishing it with attention before switching to the other.

As if that wasn't enough, his hand slid between her thighs and his callused finger stroked her, sliding between her moist lips, then using her own lube to draw circles on her clit.

She couldn't help but grind against his hand, her desire for him burning fast and furious, their days apart having made her so hungry for him.

She cried out, only to have the sound swallowed by his mouth.

"Shhh," he whispered against her lips. Their tongues engaged in a wet battle as her hands tugged at his pants.

It had been so long since she'd had him inside her. His firm length sprang free and she wrapped her hand around it, stroking it until he gasped, "Enough, or I won't make it inside you."

That would be a shame.

"Ride me, Ariel. I need to feel your cunt wrapped around my cock."

Yes. She immediately straddled him, her thighs framing his, her body poised over his shaft.

He dug his fingers into her waist as she sank down

on to his prick. She took her time lowering herself, savoring every inch as it slid in.

His fingers tightened, almost painfully, a measure of his desire. She loved it when he lost control.

"Fuck me," she whispered, knowing how the words would drive him wild.

"Ariel." His nickname for her poured from his lips as he filled her with his shaft.

She rode him as he thrust up in to her, the width of his cock stretching, the length of him pushing deep. Deeper.

Steph rocked on top of him, back and forth, each grind and thrust ramping her pleasure. Her sex clung tightly to him and she had to fight to not moan aloud. She didn't want anyone to interrupt.

Leaning forward, she changed the angle and kissed him, the mix of their hot breaths its own kind of foreplay.

"Yes," he hissed as her pussy clamped down on him. "I love you, Steph. I love you so fucking much.

"Gavin," she sighed his name as she climaxed, her channel rippling around his cock, milking him when he came in hot spurts.

Closely connected, she collapsed against him, and smiled.

He loves me.

So, why did Gavin sigh?

"What's wrong?" She tilted her face to see his.

"I wasn't supposed to seduce you."

"I rather enjoyed it."

"So did I," he hastened to reassure. "Except it wasn't part of my plan."

"What was your plan?"

"Kidnap you and take you back to my ship and then use the rope to hold you still while I proved how much I loved you."

"We can totally still do that. What are we waiting for?"

The chuckle made his body vibrate. "And this is why I fell for you. You're so fucking perfect. And here's to hoping we don't die before I get to show you how much I worship you."

"Why would we die?"

"Two words. Gunner. Lash."

Steph groaned. "Oh no. You brought the idiots?"

"Kind of."

"And if you took too long to come back out what were they supposed to do?"

"With those two, does it matter?"

"We have to get going," she said, scrambling off his lap and scrounging for clothes.

She felt no qualms about leaving her home, and even her brother and Zola.

It was time for her to move on and start a new life, with the man she loved.

If her family didn't accidentally kill him first.

CHAPTER TWENTY-FIVE

EXITING STEPH'S BEDROOM, WHICH OPENED ONTO A courtyard that he'd slipped into from the roof, Gavin tried to keep her tucked behind him.

For her, the protector in him came out full force.

But she wouldn't let him act as shield, she insisted on holding his hand and sticking by his side, and them both confronting the waiting party.

The rather large waiting party.

Zola, her braids pulled back and leaning against a stave stood beside Ronin, a big fellow with his arms crossed over his chest looking mighty forbidding.

Behind them ranged more men, a variety of ages from young to old, all hardened with flinty gazes. Her family, and they'd come to greet the man who thought he could steal their little sister/cousin.

This is gonna hurt.

Especially since he'd wager he wasn't allowed to kill them. Steph would probably get pissed if he hurt them, yet if he did nothing, they'd probably grind him to a pulp.

And this is why love hurts.

Ronin was the one to step forward and demand, "Exactly what do you think you're doing with my sister?"

Somehow, telling this beast of a man that they'd already done dirty deeds didn't seem like the best plan. However, Gavin did have something to say, so he stood tall, and smiled. "I am planning to make an honest woman of her."

"You want to marry Stephy?" Ronin frowned. He peeked at Steph then back at Gavin. "You have met her, right?"

"What's that supposed to mean?" she snapped.

"Just that you're, um, er…" Ronin stammered as she took a menacing step forward, and Gavin bit back a smile.

He patted their linked hands. "I think he's saying you tend to be feisty. But, don't worry, I like that about you."

"You do?" Ronin wasn't the only one to look surprised, but he quickly hid it behind a scowl. "What makes you think you're good enough for my sister?"

"I'm not, but I've discovered I can't live without her."

She tossed her hair. "Of course you can't. On account I'm so awesome."

That definitely got more than a few snickers from the crowd.

"If you are planning to marry her, then why sneak in to try and steal her?" Ronin still looked uncompromising.

Zola punched him in the arm. "Because it's romantic, you idiot."

Ronin rubbed his bicep and glared down at his foster mother. "Shouldn't he be asking me permission?"

"I'm asking you now. I love your sister, temper and all. Would you do me the honor of giving me permission to make her my wife?"

"Sure." Ronin shrugged.

At his nonchalant gesture, Steph screeched. "You jerk. You were fucking with him."

"Of course I was," her brother snickered. "If he wants you, he can have you. Any man good enough to be in Henderson's top five is all right in my books. Although…" His expression turned grim. "If he ever harms a hair on your head, I'll crush him." A meaty fist smacked into his open palm and an agreeing murmur went through the crowd.

Gavin didn't take offense. He understood how the other man felt. He'd kill anyone who ever hurt her, too.

"So, when are you tying the knot?" Ronin asked.

"Soon, I guess," Gavin replied.

"How soon?" Zola asked, trying to look innocent.

"Why do you care?" Steph tossed a puzzled look at the other woman.

"I might have come across a gown for you while scavenging in the islands. But with you being pregnant, it might not fit for long."

"Pregnant? What do you mean she's pregnant?" Ronin turned a thunderous gaze on Gavin. "You defiled my sister!"

"Um, Gavin, we might want to run."

Run where? He noticed the rope he'd used to climb down was gone. The other entrances through the place were blocked by bodies.

"I've got a better plan," he said as the rotating

blades of the chopper grew louder. He snaked an arm around her waist. "Trust me."

"With my life."

Overhead, a chopper appeared, noisy and whipping up loose fabric and dust. A rope dropped from it along with a hollered, "Hold on tight!"

Lash and Gunner had come to the rescue.

As Ronin's jaw dropped in disbelief, Gavin wound the cord around his forearm while Steph clung to him. They rose to the shouts of a now livid Ronin, along with the laughter of those they left behind.

"You fucking bastard. Come back here so I can beat you!" Ronin yelled.

"I think he's pissed," Gavin muttered.

Tucked close to him, Steph heard. "Ya think?"

"How long before he doesn't try to kill me?" he asked as they dangled mid-air.

"Oh, you'll always have to watch yourself. He's rather protective of me."

"In other words, sleep with one eye open. Good thing you're worth it."

"I love you, Gavin," she said, kissing him as the ladder spun.

"I love you too, Ariel." Now and forever.

THE WEDDING HAPPENED within the month. Ronin gave away the bride—who looked lovely in a white lace gown. Her groom even more handsome in a suit and no black eye, despite Ronin's threats.

Henderson paid for the party, and as a gift, laid black market sanctions on Crusty Seadog. Lash and

Gunner got laid. Cole glared at everyone who came too close to Lillie. As for the married couple?

They lived happily ever after, if a bit crazily given a pregnant Steph meant Gavin stressing about everything to the point she yelled at him. A lot.

But that was okay. Theirs was a love that could handle a little mayhem and torture. As for the baby on the way? Terrified the fuck out of him, but he already loved him/her.

This is my family. And as it turned out, real men did cry when that family got bigger.

END

RONIN'S STORY IS COMING SOON IN GOING STRAIGHT. ALSO WATCH OUT FOR SOME MENAGE ACTION WITH LASH AND GUNNER IN DOUBLE TROUBLE.

More info at: SuzanneLangRomance.com

www.ingramcontent.com/pod-product-compliance
Lightning Source LLC
Chambersburg PA
CBHW030913060726
47591CB00005B/1523